"I'm, um, not interrupting anything, am I?"

Mollie shrugged a slender shoulder. "I was just having breakfast."

Some of his thoughts must have shown on his face. Mollie's eyes widened. "Oh, my—" Reaching out, she socked him in the shoulder just like she'd done when she was a kid. "It was a *first* date, Zeke!"

"I know, but—" She'd looked so gorgeous the night before. What man wouldn't have wanted to take her to bed?

"But what? Oh, that's right! You know me so well! You must have realized I was out for some kind of wild affair!"

Wild affair.

The words kept bouncing off his stunned brain in more and more dangerous combinations. *Mollie... affair. Mollie...wild.*

Truth was, she looked a little wild right then. With her red hair ablaze from the morning sunlight streaming through the lace-curtained windows. With sapphire sparks flying from her eyes. With her chest heaving beneath the black cotton tank top.

But he didn't think of Mollie that way. He couldn't.

* * *

FUREVER YOURS: Finding forever homes— and hearts!—has never been so easy.

Dear Reader,

Thank you for picking up *Not Just the Girl Next Door*, the third book in Special Edition's Furever Yours series! When the editors at Harlequin approached me about writing for this series, I was thrilled to be included—both as an author and as a dog lover.

The heroine of this book, dog trainer Mollie McFadden, immediately spoke to me. She's a little shy, a little awkward and more comfortable around her furry friends than around people! But she has a big heart—especially when it comes to her foster dogs, Charlie and Chief, and her secret crush, Zeke Harper.

Zeke Harper is a hero who takes responsibility seriously, including looking out for Mollie, his childhood friend. He's always around to help with fixing up her house or to hang out together with her dogs, but he isn't ready to see that the girl next door is all grown up.

Mollie knows Zeke could be her perfect match, but what will it take to prove to him that falling in love with his best friend isn't such a far-fetched idea after all?

I hope you enjoy *Not Just the Girl Next Door* and that you'll look for the other books in the Furever Yours series written by my fellow Special Edition authors—Melissa Senate, Teri Wilson, Karen Rose Smith, Kathy Douglass and Christy Jeffries.

Happy Tails!

Stacy Connelly

Not Just the Girl Next Door

—

Stacy Connelly

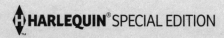

HARLEQUIN® SPECIAL EDITION

Special thanks and acknowledgment are given to Stacy Connelly for her contribution to the Furever Yours series.

Recycling programs
for this product may
not exist in your area.

ISBN-13: 978-1-335-57375-9

Not Just the Girl Next Door

Copyright © 2019 by Harlequin Books S.A.

HARLEQUIN®
www.Harlequin.com

Printed in U.S.A.

Stacy Connelly has dreamed of publishing books since writing stories about a girl and her horse. Eventually, boys made it onto the page as she discovered a love of romance novels. She is thrilled that her novel *Once Upon a Wedding* was recently turned into a movie titled *Christmas Wedding Planner*.

Stacy lives in Arizona with her two spoiled dogs. She loves to hear from readers at stacyconnelly@cox.net, at stacyconnelly.com or on Facebook.

Books by Stacy Connelly

Harlequin Special Edition

Hillcrest House

The Best Man Takes a Bride
How to Be a Blissful Bride

The Pirelli Brothers

His Secret Son
Romancing the Rancher
Small-Town Cinderella
Daddy Says, "I Do!"
Darcy and the Single Dad
Her Fill-In Fiancé

Temporary Boss...Forever Husband
The Wedding She Always Wanted
Once Upon a Wedding
All She Wants for Christmas

Visit the Author Profile page
at Harlequin.com for more titles.

To the real-life shelter workers dedicated to
finding forever homes for the animals in their care...
Thank you!

To Susan Litman and Gail Chasan
for thinking of me!

And to my Shadow... I miss you, baby girl.

Chapter One

Mollie McFadden scooted closer to the good-looking guy in the corner. "Hey, handsome. How'd a fellow like you end up in a place like this?"

Soulful brown eyes glanced in her direction, then quickly away, but Mollie didn't let that deter her. She had a reputation for winning over strong, silent types. "I bet you've got a story to tell, don't you?"

Again a slight flicker of eyelids, this time followed by a big sigh.

"A heartbreaking one, too, huh?" She inched a little closer but kept her hands to herself even though her heart ached to offer the comfort he obviously craved. "Bet you're feeling lost and abandoned and alone."

Her pulse skipped a beat as he shifted. He might have simply been looking for a more comfortable position, but she didn't miss how he settled a little closer to her. "But you have to believe things are going to get better."

He let out a huff that sounded more than a little doubtful. "I'm telling you, it will. Look at all Spring Forest has been through in the last few months, including a tornado, of all things!"

Maybe she was reading too much into body language, but Mollie swore a slight shudder ran through his solid frame. "The storm was pretty scary, wasn't it? But in Spring Forest, people really help each other out. You'll see if you just give us a chance. In fact..." she leaned closer to whisper "...something tells me you might even find your perfect match."

A pair of dark eyebrows rose at that. "I know, I know. It seems hard to believe now, but I have a good feeling about this."

And that feeling grew and bloomed and warmed her heart into a melting puddle of goo as the rescue dog named Chief slowly lowered his chin to rest against her jean-clad thigh.

Reaching out, she gently placed her hand on the soft ruff of fur at his neck. "We're going to find a great home for you." Though she'd worked with plenty of pound puppies during her years volunteering at the animal shelter, Mollie's throat clogged with tears as she promised, "The very best home."

The Whitaker sisters, affectionately known by the nicknames Birdie and Bunny, had asked Mollie to come to the Furever Paws Animal Rescue to meet with Chief. As a dog trainer, she worked with many dogs—from purebreds to shelter mutts. Shy pups like Chief, though, were the ones she had a soft spot for. Most canines were outgoing, adventurous and loving by nature. To see one so trapped by fear, cowering in the back of his kennel, broke her heart.

Adopters were all too likely to pass up diamonds in

the rough like Chief. "Not this time, boy," she promised. "We're going to break you out of your shell and show the world how fabulous you are."

Mollie cringed a little at the familiar words. They mirrored the bold, confident vow her friend Amanda Sylvester had made. Only Amanda hadn't been talking about a four-legged companion. She'd been talking about *Mollie*.

But Mollie didn't care about the whole world seeing her as special…just one particular guy who unfortunately only saw her as his best friend's little sister.

Chief made a small sound, a mix between a whine and a bark, definitely punctuated by a question mark at the end.

"Oh, don't you worry," Mollie insisted as she shoved thoughts of her pathetic love life from her mind. "The odds are way more in your favor."

With his striking black-and-tan coloring, medium build and short fur, Chief had the outward makings of an easily adoptable dog. All he needed was a bit of confidence and adopters would no longer walk by his kennel before he had a chance to catch their eye.

"Something tells me you're smart, too." Even though he was a mix, shepherds were generally regarded as one of the most intelligent breeds. "I bet we can even teach you some tricks, like—"

Mollie didn't get a chance to tell Chief about the joys of fetch. A sudden crash shook the window. With a startled yelp, the dog scrambled to his paws and scurried to his corner.

Mollie glared at the wall as if she could see through to the construction going on outside. She'd asked Birdie to take Chief out of his kennel and into one of the visitation rooms. Though the furnishings were all secondhand donations, the worn brown leather sofas, mismatched end tables and floral area rug had all the touches of a typical living room. Mollie wanted Chief to associate the home-like environment with a safe and happy place.

Something she was going to have an even harder time accomplishing now. Mollie took a deep breath and forced her own tense muscles to relax. Getting frustrated wouldn't help. She often felt her own dog, Arti, could tell what kind of a day she'd had before she even walked through the door and kicked off her shoes. She didn't want poor Chief thinking she was upset with him.

But despite her best efforts, the loud noise had erased the small progress she'd made. Curled in the corner with his nose practically tucked behind his hind leg, the dog refused to respond.

Swallowing her disappointment, but reminding herself that changing behavior took time, she slipped from the room and walked down the long hallway toward the main lobby. Thanks to a recent fund-raiser, the Whitaker sisters had plans to spruce up the small space, including updating the furniture and adding some color to the plain beige walls and a new stain treatment to the concrete floors.

For now, the main bright spot was the small gift shop off to the side where a rainbow of leashes and collars lined the walls in a variety of styles and sizes. The store also offered a selection of bowls and toys and beds. Everything an adopter might need when taking home a new furry friend.

One of the shelter volunteers was working the front desk, phone tucked against her shoulder as she jotted some notes. "I'm sorry, can you say that again?" the girl asked, pressing her free hand against her ear as the high-pitched whine of a saw filled the air.

Mollie pushed one of the glass doors open and stepped out onto the front porch. The scent of freshly cut wood drifted on the midmorning breeze, and she followed the strident, no-nonsense sound of Birdie Whitaker's voice around the side of the building. The sixtysomething shelter co-owner, dressed in a denim jumpsuit over a long-sleeved blue T-shirt, was known for working twice as hard as most people half her age.

"Is everything okay?" Mollie asked after the woman finished her conversation with the construction foreman.

Birdie shook her head. "I can't wait for these repairs to be over. I hope the work will start to speed up now that Rebekah's applied for a grant," she said, speaking of the shelter's new director.

The brown roof and dark gray siding weren't much to look at, but the prominently displayed logo—the silhouette of a dog and a cat within a large heart—spoke to the shelter's main purpose. And, as always, Birdie focused on what mattered most. "We hope to use that money to expand the kennels so we can house more animals, plus create an outdoor space for the cats and a dog run."

"The changes are going to be a huge benefit to the shelter," Mollie agreed. And, more importantly, to the animals. Birdie and Bunny were such amazing advocates for the furry friends in their care—always striving to treat them as potential pets rather than as unwanted strays.

"But now for the reason why I asked you to come to Furever Paws today. What do you think about Chief?"

"He's such a sweet dog, but he's so skittish." After explaining her minor success with the dog and then

Chief's reaction to the noise outside, Mollie asked, "Is there anyone here he's bonded with?"

If ever a dog needed a foster home, it was Chief. Between the volunteers and a stream of adopters coming through, not to mention the varied mix of other animals, shelters could be stressful. Add in the construction noise, and kennel life had to be terrifying for the poor dog.

"Well," the older woman mused, "there is someone." Spotting another volunteer walking up the gravel parking lot with a gorgeous yellow Lab, Birdie said, "Excuse me for one moment."

After speaking to the young woman, Birdie returned to Mollie's side. "Come with me. There's something you should see."

Leading the way back down the hall toward the visitation room, Birdie stopped at the large viewing window. As she stepped up to the glass, Mollie looked for Chief in his corner, but the dog wasn't there. Instead, he was sitting in the middle of the room, gazing adoringly at a gorgeous blonde.

"He doesn't even look like the same dog," Mollie said, amazed by the change in his demeanor. Though his ears were still back and his head bowed in typical submissive behavior, Chief had stopped shaking. She might have even seen a hint of a tail wag across the linoleum floor. "Who is that in there with him?"

Birdie grinned. "That is Charlie."

"Charlie." Mollie took a closer look at the large dog circling the room with her nose pressed to the ground and her tail swishing through the air. "Isn't she the dog Claire and Matt were considering for his niece before Ellie ended up falling in love with Sparkle?"

Claire Asher, a teacher at the local middle school

and fellow volunteer, had recently gotten engaged to her one-time high school sweetheart, Matt Fielding. The two of them had reunited while helping Ellie train Sparkle.

"Yes. Matt's sister wanted a smaller dog. I'm starting to think that might be just as well, seeing how Chief is so attached to Charlie. Bunny is hoping we can find someone to adopt them as a pair, but with larger dogs, that's not as likely."

Adopting them out together would be ideal. So, too, would fostering them as a pair. Not that Mollie had arrived at the shelter with any intention of fostering Chief. She was supposed to be there only to offer her assessment. But hadn't she known within minutes of meeting the shy dog that the shelter wasn't the best place for him? As she watched Charlie lower her chest almost to the floor with her tail wagging wildly behind her in a classic play bow, Mollie knew having the happy-go-lucky Lab on her side would make working with Chief much easier.

Mollie sighed. She'd never been able to turn away from a dog in need. She smiled in memory of her first dog, Shadow. Her parents had never allowed animals in the house, so the stray that she and Zeke Harper rescued had ended up living at his house a few doors down. Mollie had spent almost as much time over at the Harpers' as she had at her own home.

Of course, not all of that had been about spending time with Shadow...

Pushing the thought from her mind, Mollie turned her focus to the shy shepherd. "Chief needs a quieter environment and to spend one-on-one time with a human to get over his fear."

"So you'll take them—I mean, him," Birdie corrected quickly.

But Mollie wasn't fooled. Knowing it had likely been the older woman's plan all along, she sighed. "I'll take them both."

Mollie knew she'd made the right decision as soon as she loaded Charlie and Chief into her SUV. Chief balked when she led him toward the back hatch, lowering his head and thrashing against the leash. Mollie had anticipated having to struggle to get the good-sized dog into one of the crates she'd borrowed from the shelter. Charlie, however, sailed over the lowered tailgate and settled right in. Clearly afraid of being left behind, Chief followed suit.

"You're going to be my right-hand dog, aren't you, Charlie?" Mollie asked as she left Spring Forest behind and headed toward the rural outskirts north of the small North Carolina town.

Four years ago, when Mollie had been looking for a home of her own, she'd known she wanted a place in the country. Dog training could be on the noisy side, and she hadn't wanted any next-door neighbors to complain. Plus, she knew she'd need plenty of outdoor space for distance training as well as agility work.

Her tiny house on its large lot was perfect.

She wrinkled her nose a little at the thought. Okay, it was perfect for the dogs. She still had some work to do—maybe even a lot of work to do—before the place would be perfect for her. And she really did have a plan for the needed repairs and improvements and upgrades. Somehow, though, time tended to get away from her, which led to dozens of half-finished projects and an overwhelming number of idea boards on Pinterest.

"Don't you worry, though," she told the dogs. "You guys come first."

She'd get around to those repairs soon enough and—

Mollie braked a bit harder than she'd intended as she caught sight of a familiar sleek black sedan parked off to the side of her house. Her heart instantly skipped a beat. She hadn't expected to see Zeke today. She'd texted him after Birdie asked her to swing by the shelter. So for him to show up unannounced, at a time when he knew she wouldn't be around, only meant one thing.

Her pulse picked up as she opened the driver-side door, and Mollie had to remind herself that she was annoyed with him. How many times did they have to have this conversation?

"Hey, Moll." Walking around the side of her house like he owned it, Zeke Harper greeted her with a smile. "How did it go at the shelter?"

Mollie tried to glare at him. She really did. But as he lifted a muscled arm to wipe the sheen of sweat off his forehead, annoyance wasn't exactly the emotion sending a blast of heat through her body. Dressed in a navy T-shirt and well-worn jeans with—heaven help her—a leather tool belt around his narrow hips, Zeke Harper looked more like the hot host of a DIY show than like the respected psychologist he was.

Trying to keep her voice, her blood pressure and her hormones from blasting sky high, she asked, "What are you doing here, Zeke?"

He hitched a thumb over one broad shoulder. "I thought I'd get a jump on replacing those rotted steps on the back porch." A smile he didn't try all that hard to hide tugged at his lips. "You were off to such a good start, tearing them out like you did."

Mollie's face heated. She'd felt quite proud of herself as she'd torn out the rotting wood steps, risers and stringers. Since then, she'd made several unsuccessful attempts at cutting the new stringers but could never quite get the angle right. So she had moved on to another project and contented herself with knowing she was getting her lunge work in every time she came in from the backyard.

"I was going to finish them," she said.

"Sure you were, kid," Zeke said happily as he threw an arm around her shoulders. "But what are friends for?"

Mollie cringed a little, enough so Zeke noticed and quickly removed his arm. "Sorry, I guess I am kind of sweaty."

"You know I'm not afraid to get dirty," Mollie challenged.

As their gazes met, for a brief second the atmosphere around them seem to change, to shimmer with an electric charge like the air right before a storm. His hazel eyes, normally so full of teasing and laughter, darkened, and Mollie's heart fluttered in her chest.

But then he blinked, and whatever she *thought* she'd seen disappeared. "You had a three foot drop-off at the edge of the porch. That's not safe."

Overprotective concern. Now *that* emotion she immediately recognized and the curious flutter sank to her stomach like a stone.

Kid, she reminded herself as she swallowed hard. *Friend.* That was how Zeke thought of her. The little sister he'd never wanted.

He had teasingly dubbed her with the title long ago, and even though she'd never thought of him as a big brother, a part of her clung to the designation like a shield. Anything to keep the man she'd fallen in love with years ago from ever learning about her hopeless crush.

"You could at least wait for me to ask for help first," she argued.

"I would." He pinned her with a knowing look. "But you never ask."

Maybe she did have a habit of digging deeper when she was already in over her head. But she wasn't a kid anymore, and the woman in Mollie longed for the day when Zeke Harper would see her as someone other than his best friend's little sister…always in need of rescue.

Chapter Two

"Two dogs?" Zeke demanded as he followed Mollie around the side gate to her backyard. Though her property extended far beyond the fence line, the wooden structure that surrounded the large grassy area was one of the first remodeling projects he'd helped her with.

Before taking on the leaky faucets. Before putting in the new water heater. Before tearing out the decades-old carpet. Because the fence was important to the dogs and the dogs were more important to Mollie than anything.

He admired her huge heart when it came to the animals, he really did. But he was starting to worry that she was dedicating too much of her life to the dogs she rescued and the ones she trained.

"Your text said that you were going to the shelter to evaluate a dog. You never said anything about bringing two of them home with you."

"I *did* go to evaluate him." She tossed the words,

along with her reddish-blond curls, over her shoulder as she glanced back at him. "And my evaluation was that Chief needed to be in a foster home and out of a kennel."

Mollie had introduced him to both dogs—the happy, playful seventy-pound puppy named Charlie and the shy, scared Chief.

The poor guy did look terrified. He'd been cowering in the back of the crate in Mollie's SUV, and it had taken quite a bit of coaxing from Mollie and some encouraging barks from Charlie to get him to come out. And even then, he'd crouched so low that his belly was practically brushing against the grass.

"Look, I get it, but don't you think this is a lot to take on? Between the house, volunteering at Furever Paws, your job, your own dog…" He waved a hand to the house, trying not to cringe at the sound of Arti howling like mad inside. Mollie loved the long-eared hound like a kid, but Zeke wasn't sure he'd ever met a goofier, clumsier, crazier dog.

"I can do this, Zeke. The house is fine. I'm perfectly capable of handling my volunteer work and my job, and Arti is, well, Arti." Unleashing both of the new dogs to explore a backyard filled with various dog toys and agility equipment, Mollie said, "I'll introduce the three of them later today, but I'm sure they'll get along."

Though Zeke didn't dare say so out loud, it wasn't the house, the shelter, her job or her dogs he was worried about. It was Mollie herself. She worked hard, probably too hard, and while he knew she kept in good physical shape—she couldn't possibly keep up with the rigors of dog training and agility if she didn't—she spent too much time alone with only canine companionship.

But whenever he encouraged her to go out more often, Mollie would only laugh. "What can I say?" she'd joked more than once. "I get along better with animals than I do with people. I wear my 'crazy dog lady' title with pride!"

Zeke didn't think Mollie was crazy—not as a friend and not as a psychologist. He had noticed, though, that she'd isolated herself more and more over the past two years. That worried him. When he saw a problem, his first instinct was to find a solution, and he quickly decided Mollie needed to get out more, to go on a date or two. She'd need a bit of encouragement, of course, which was where he came in. Fixing her up would be no different than fixing her back steps.

Okay, maybe it was a little different...

Certainly his track record with power tools was better than his own success when it came to relationships. And that included the time in shop class when he'd slipped while working with a circular saw and needed twenty-two stitches. At least he'd only tried cutting his fool hand off.

Lilah Fairchild had done her best to rip out his heart.

But Mollie was nothing like his ex-fiancée. She was sweet and kind and funny, and Zeke didn't like the idea of her being alone.

And Patrick wouldn't have, either.

Zeke took a deep breath and refocused his attention on Mollie and the new dogs as Charlie raced over at full speed and jumped up, planted a pair of muddy paws right on Mollie's chest and dropped a tennis ball at her feet. Zeke knew plenty of women—Lilah included—who would have been annoyed. But Mollie merely laughed and bent to pick up the slobber-covered green felt. "Somebody needs a few lessons in the proper way to greet people, but look what a smart girl you are to find a ball!"

The silly Lab basked in the praise, tail wagging her entire body, pink tongue hanging out the side of her mouth. Zeke wasn't surprised. Mollie had always known how to encourage him, too, how to cheer him up like she had in the days following his broken engagement.

Lilah wasn't good enough for you. You deserve someone so much better.

Mollie deserved the best, which would make finding the right guy for her a tall order. Not that plenty of guys wouldn't be willing. Even though Mollie wasn't the type to waste time messing around with her hair or piling on makeup, she had a fresh-faced beauty. With her reddish curls, blue-green eyes and freckled skin, he'd always thought she was cute.

He watched as Mollie tried to engage the dog in a game of fetch, but Charlie clearly had other ideas. Like playing keep-away by racing around the yard, prized ball clutched in her drooling jaws. The dog zigged every time Mollie zagged, and her laughter grabbed hold of something inside his chest.

Cute? Hell, she was gorgeous.

The late-afternoon sun brought out the blaze of golden highlights in her hair. Her royal blue Best Friends T-shirt showed off her toned arms and the thin material hugged her breasts. Her jeans were well-worn and faded, one of the back pockets partially torn off and flapping against a perfectly rounded backside. The tattered square seemed to taunt him to reach out and give a tug, and he didn't think it was any latent OCD tendencies that had his palms sweating.

Almost as if sensing the wayward direction of his thoughts, Charlie charged toward Zeke, grass churning beneath her paws, and launched straight at his midsection. He might have withstood the blow if Chief hadn't wandered up behind him, close enough that the back of his knees connected with the dog's sturdy body as he stumbled backward, upending him as easily as the stupid prank-playing jocks back in high school had.

He landed flat on his back with a grunt, squinting up at the bright sky overhead. The fragrant grass was cool through the material of his T-shirt, but not cool enough to keep the heat of embarrassment from sinking into his skin.

"And to think, I didn't even have to train them to do that. Such natural talent!"

"Very funny," Zeke grumbled, glaring up at Mollie's smiling face as she moved to block out the sun. Not that her smile was any less bright or less effective at warming the blood pumping through his veins.

She held out a slender hand. Determined to regain control of his baffling desire, Zeke reached up, caught her by the wrist and pulled too hard…just like he would have done back when they were kids.

Mollie lost her balance, her startled shriek cutting off with a soft "Umph," as she tumbled down to the ground beside him. Charlie, thinking this was another new game, nosed her way in between them, bouncing the disgusting ball off Zeke's forehead before trying to lick the two of them to death.

Chuckling as he lay on the ground, it was like he was a kid again, running wild with Mollie, Patrick and Shadow, and all seemed right in his world once more. Mollie was still the ponytailed, tagalong kid he remembered, the one who always had been and always would be his friend.

But then she sat up, shaking her hair back with a toss of her head as she leaned over him. Time jumped forward from one heartbeat to the next, and suddenly she was all woman. The smell of fresh-cut grass mingled with the wildflower scent of her skin, and Zeke's body clenched in reaction.

The hazy mist of nostalgia burned away under the unexpected blaze of lust, followed quickly by an equally scorching wave of guilt. Mollie wasn't that little girl anymore. The dog dancing around them was Charlie, not Shadow, and Patrick was—

Cutting off the thought, Zeke pushed to his feet. Charlie sat a few yards away, the ball at her feet, and if ever a canine could look smug, she did. "You've got your work cut out for you with that one," he said, his tone sharper than he'd intended.

Mollie frowned up at him as she slowly stood. She brushed at the blades of grass clinging to the back of her jeans, and Zeke had to force his gaze away. "It's been too long since you've had a dog. You've forgotten how much energy a puppy has to burn."

"I haven't forgotten."

Acting as though she hadn't heard him, Mollie said, "I can think of a really easy way to remedy that."

They'd had this discussion plenty of times, and the familiarity of the argument helped settle his unease. "I don't think so."

"I don't understand why not. You know how much you loved Shadow."

"I did. She was the greatest. But you did the heavy lifting." Mollie had been over at his parents' house all of the time—willing to walk the dog, play fetch with her, keep her well groomed.

"Taking care of someone you love is never work."

Zeke wasn't sure why his eyes automatically went to the newly built stairs leading to Mollie's back porch.

That had been a lot of work, but he'd been more than willing to do it because…because…

"It's a responsibility," he argued, not even realizing he'd said the words out loud until Mollie started talking again.

"Owning any kind of pet is a responsibility." She shot him a grin. "But you've always been a responsible guy."

He *was* a responsible guy, and by default, Mollie was his responsibility. Whether she liked it or not. He would never admit it, but a part of him was glad that Mollie had a stubborn tendency to resist his efforts. Any show of gratitude would only have added to his feelings of guilt—and Zeke already had plenty of that where the McFadden siblings were concerned.

Years ago, Zeke had made his best friend a promise. Straight out of boot camp and ready for a tour that would take him overseas, Patrick McFadden had asked Zeke to look out for his little sister.

Zeke had immediately agreed. He and Patrick had grown up as neighbors in an affluent, historic section of Spring Forest. Patrick had been the closest thing Zeke had to a brother. And just as Zeke and Patrick had always been best friends, meeting up after school, playing sports, exploring the woods around Spring Forest on the weekends, Mollie had always been the kid sister wanting to tag along. Looking out for her came as naturally as hanging out with Patrick.

Both men knew Mollie had a big heart—maybe too big. She was always willing to think the best of people, to give anyone who asked a second, third, fourth chance. The last thing either of them wanted was for someone to take advantage of her giving, caring nature.

With his friend answering the call of duty and willing to risk his life in service to his country, Zeke didn't want Patrick to have to worry about his little sister back home. So Zeke had made his friend that promise.

And then, two years ago, Mollie had shown up at his door, her bright eyes ravaged by tears, to tell him that Patrick was never coming home.

His best friend was dead, and the promise Zeke had made—along with the reminder of Patrick's final visit home—weighed on Zeke so heavily that the crushing pressure on his chest made it hard to breathe.

He looked down, startled by the cold press of a nose against his hand followed by the familiar weight and warmth of a sturdy canine body leaning against his leg. Reaching down, he ran his palm over Charlie's silky golden head, taking comfort in the easy, quiet companionship.

"You need a new best friend."

His heart cramped a bit at the softly spoken words, and he looked up to find Mollie watching him, her gentle soul reflected in her blue-green eyes. Logic told him neither she nor the dog by his side could possibly know what he'd been thinking. But from his own experiences with Shadow and with the service dogs at the veterans' support group where he volunteered, he knew how intuitive animals could be.

And as for Mollie… Patrick was a tie that would always bind them together. Zeke didn't need to tell her he was thinking about his friend. Not when Patrick was always there between the two of them.

The steps were perfect. The raw wood was sanded to a smooth finish awaiting the stain or paint of her choosing. Mollie had no doubt that each step and rise was strictly to code and not a single degree off.

But that was Zeke. All straight lines and precise measurements. His massive toolbox lay open at the top of the stairs. Inside, each red plastic section held a specific size of nail, screw, nut or bolt. Everything properly labeled and carefully maintained, and nothing like her junk drawer, which held a random mishmash of items that may as well have escaped from the island of lost tools.

"You could have waited for me, you know. I would have liked to see how you figured out how to cut the stringers...just in case."

"It's not that hard."

She held up a hand as Zeke went on about maximum riser height and tread depth, cutting him off by saying, "I get it. You're brilliant."

And he was. Zeke was the smartest person she knew, and not just book smart. If there was anything he wanted to learn—and Zeke tended to want to learn *everything*—he could pick up a how-to book or watch a few online videos and know all there was to know about cutting stringers, building a fence or replacing a faucet.

"You don't have to worry." He stomped a booted foot against the lowest tread. "Trust me, these suckers are solid. They aren't going anywhere."

"Well, no. Not unless I tear them out again."

"Tear them out? Why would you do that?"

"Because they're too perfect!" The old steps, though lacking in structural integrity, had made up for their rough, splintered surfaces with character. They'd had knots and dents and a weathered finish that matched up with the rest of her house. "I'm going to have to replace the deck, the door, the back half of the house to try to get everything to look half as good as your steps."

Zeke only grinned. "Sounds like I have my work cut out for me the next few weekends."

"No, Zeke. You don't. It's my house. My responsibility."

For a brief second, a shadow seemed to cross over his handsome features before he offered her a confident smile. "Of course it is, but that doesn't mean I can't help out around here, does it? How else am I going to pay you back for all the delicious meals you make me?"

Mollie hardly considered herself any kind of gourmet chef, but she did like to eat. She also liked to cook, especially if it meant cooking for Zeke.

Though if there was any truth to the old adage *the way to a man's heart is through his stomach*, Zeke would have fallen for her back when she was in the eighth grade and he ate all the cookies she'd made for a bake sale.

"You can't tell me you don't have some mouth-watering meal already started."

"I may have thrown the ingredients for chili into the slow cooker before I left this morning."

His gaze narrowed. "What kind of chili?"

Mollie rolled her eyes. "Tofu," she said. "What do you think?"

Crossing his arms over his chest, he said, "I think you'd better be lying."

"It's ground sirloin." Though she did occasionally like to switch things up with a white chicken chili or ground turkey, she knew better than to lean too far in the healthy food direction.

Zeke had complained more than once that the tall, model-thin women he dated in Raleigh loved dressing up and going out to dinner and yet refused to order anything more than a small salad and ridiculously priced bottled water. He swore he broke up with his last girlfriend after she invited him over for pizza and then served vegetable toppings and soy cheese on a cauliflower crust.

He didn't have to worry about that with Mollie on any score. She hated cauliflower and loved thick-crust pepperoni pizza covered in mozzarella. She was not tall, she was not thin and no one would mistake her for a model.

All of which made her perfect for Zeke. The perfect buddy, that was.

Mollie swallowed a sigh as she stomped up the expertly crafted steps and led the way into the kitchen. She was greeted by the smell of slow-cooking beef, onions and garlic, and by the exuberant head to tail wagging of her black-and-tan coonhound.

"Hey, baby girl! I missed you, too." Mollie reached down to run her hands over the dog's floppy ears. After the initial greeting, Arti immediately set about sniffing every inch of her denim jeans. By the time the dog was finished, Mollie was certain the hound had figured out every person she'd talked to and every dog she'd stopped to pet in the hours since she'd been gone from the house.

Fortunately, Arti was not the jealous type. Mollie only wished she could say the same when Zeke bent down to say hello and her dog had the fantasy-inspiring pleasure of throwing herself against that broad chest, nuzzling his neck and even stealing a quick kiss.

"Crazy dog!"

Of course, Zeke's laughter as he pushed Arti away and wiped at his mouth with the back of his hand was very much the response Mollie anticipated if she ever acted on that fantasy.

Crazy Mollie...

Zeke had been over for dinner at her house often

enough that she didn't need to tell him where to find the soup bowls, glasses or spoons. They moved around each other in the small space with Mollie ducking beneath his arm as he reached into an upper cabinet, side-stepping his broad form as she pulled the toppings from the refrigerator and swatting his hand when he tried to sample a bite of chili straight off the wooden spoon.

It was all so easy and natural, and Mollie had years of experience ignoring the delicious shiver that raced through her body at the incidental touches—the brush of her arm against his chest, the warmth of his hand at her shoulder as he leaned close to inhale the spicy aroma of the simmering chili.

"That smells amazing," he complimented her, and Mollie couldn't help thinking the same thing—about Zeke.

She wanted nothing more than to turn in the circle of his arms and breathe him in. To soak in the warm and spicy scent of his aftershave combined with summer sunshine and cedar. To have him look at her the way, well, the way he was currently looking at her chili. Like he wanted to eat *her* up with a spoon.

"Just one bite?" he cajoled. "Please…"

His warm breath teased her ear, and a shiver ran down her spine. With her legs as weak as if she'd just completed a five-mile run through the mountains with Arti, it was all Mollie could do not to melt into a puddle at his feet.

Instead, she gave him a playful jab in the ribs with her elbow. "Finish setting the table and pour our drinks, would you? I might work with animals, but we're going to sit down and eat like civilized people."

Her parents had never been pet friendly, and when she had announced she wanted to train dogs as a profession, they'd reacted as though she'd announced she planned to don animal skins, eat raw meat and live in the wild. Maybe running around with a bunch of dogs and having a layer of dog hair—and occasionally doggie drool—covering her clothes was not the most glamorous of careers. But she was *good* at training dogs.

Zeke's low chuckle, though, only served as another challenge to just how uncivilized Mollie was feeling at the moment. Fortunately, he backed away before she could make a total fool out of herself.

Shoring up her trembling legs, she carried the pot of chili over to the oak table and set it amid the bowls of sour cream, green onions, shredded cheese and sliced jalapeños.

After digging into the chili like he hadn't had a good meal in ages, Zeke asked, "How are the repairs going at the shelter?"

"Already underway, thanks to the money made at the fund-raiser last month." Mollie had operated a booth at the event, promoting her own business as well as bringing attention to the shelter and its needs. Zeke had volunteered, as well, helping her set up and drawing a fair share of female attention to the booth.

"And the Whitaker sisters told me that Rebekah Taylor, the new shelter director, has applied for a grant, not only for repairs but also for expanding the shelter."

"That must be a challenge, to start a new job while the shelter is undergoing construction repairs."

Mollie nodded. "I would think so, but if the grant comes through, the tornado might just end up a blessing in disguise."

She looked up in time to find Zeke watching her with a hint of an amused smile on his handsome face. "What?" she asked defensively, glancing down at her

T-shirt to make sure she hadn't somehow ended up with half her dinner dribbled down the front. No chili stains, but Mollie winced a little at the muddy paw prints she'd failed to notice earlier.

Great, just great.

"Only you would find a silver lining in a tornado."

Heat bloomed in Mollie's cheeks. Growing up, her parents had often warned her about the folly of viewing the world through rose-colored glasses. "You think I'm naive."

Zeke shook his head. "I think you're amazing. Chief and Charlie are the luckiest dogs in the world to have you in their corner."

The words took Mollie's breath away. "Zeke... that's—" She had to clear the emotional lump in her throat before finishing in a rush. "That's the nicest thing anyone has ever said to me."

"It's true." Reaching out, he grasped her hand in his as he gazed into her eyes.

And even though they had touched thousands of times in the years they had known each other—everything from teasing shoves and friendly hugs to clinging to each other beside her brother's grave—this felt different.

Suddenly *everything* felt different.

She could feel the warmth from Zeke's hand radiating up her arm and leaving a delicious trail of goose bumps in its wake. She could hear every beat of her heart, every bated breath she took, magnified in her head. Zeke's hazel eyes had never seemed so rich, so warm.

"It hit me out in the backyard earlier..."

"It did?" The words escaped in a Minnie Mouse–like squeak, but Mollie didn't care.

Zeke nodded. "You're such an amazing woman, Mollie. It makes no sense to me that some lucky guy hasn't come along to sweep you off your feet."

Oh... Oh! It was finally happening. After so many years of dreaming, so many years silently hoping. "Well—" Mollie swallowed "—you've probably guessed by now that I've been waiting—"

"And that's just the thing. You shouldn't have to wait. Not anymore."

"No," she agreed. "Not anymore. I'm ready, Zeke, I am."

Mollie had fallen for him when she was only a kid, on the day they'd rescued Shadow together. And, yes, back then, she had been too young for him. Even as an awkward, lovestruck teenager, she'd been too young. But that was then. Now, a four-year age difference meant nothing. Now, she was a woman and for Zeke to finally see her that way—

"I know. That's why I want to fix you up with one of my friends."

Chapter Three

"Wait, what?" Mollie yanked her hand away and jerked back so quickly, she nearly upended her chair. Barely catching herself before she could tumble over backward, she stared across the table. "You wanna what?"

"I was thinking that I could set you up on a date. You know, with one of the guys from the basketball league. Several of them are single and—look, Mollie, what I'm trying to say is that you're a great girl, a great catch."

Right. Which is why he'd just tossed her overboard.

Pushing away from the table, she grabbed her bowl of half-eaten chili and stalked over to the kitchen counter. Her face burning in humiliation, Mollie couldn't bear to look at Zeke. Leave it to her to read his words so completely wrong!

When it came to dogs, she could interpret every tail wag, every raised ruff, every ear flick. But with people?

She didn't know what was worse. That she'd so stupidly fooled herself into thinking he was interested or that he thought she was so desperate that he had to set her up on some kind of pity date.

Barely restraining the urge to throw the dishes into the sink—or right at Zeke—Mollie set the bowl on the counter and marched back to the table to face him. "This isn't like your coming over here and working on my house without my permission. I don't need you to fix my love life!"

But Zeke didn't give up easily. Especially not when he was sure that big brain of his was right. "Mollie, this isn't about fixing anything. It's about letting me help you."

She let out a low growl that would have done King, her most aggressive dog to date, proud. Instead of backing off, though, Zeke circled the table, clearly not the least bit intimidated. But then again, King had been a ten-pound Chihuahua.

Reaching out, Zeke caught her shoulders in his wide hands. As mad as she was, that moment earlier—when she'd so foolishly let herself hope, let herself believe— had unleashed something inside her. All the barriers she'd built up over the years were suddenly gone.

She wasn't a kid, and she wasn't his little sister. She was a grown woman, and she wanted Zeke to hold her, to kiss her, to love her as only a man could love a woman.

"Zeke—"

But even though everything had changed for Mollie, nothing had for Zeke.

"I know you always tell me you like dogs better than people," he was saying with a smile, "but it will do you good to go out and meet someone new. And, hey, if it would make things easier, we could always go on a double date."

"You're seeing someone?" Mollie's chest cramped at the thought as she stepped away from his embrace.

Recently, Zeke had mostly dated women he met in Raleigh. Mollie always told herself she was glad. She didn't want to see firsthand how smart, how sophisticated, how sexy those women were in comparison to her. And she feared the day when Zeke might actually find a woman he saw as The One. A smart, sexy, sophisticated woman who knew better than to serve him vegan pizza.

Two years ago, that worst-case scenario nightmare had seemed all too close to coming true when he'd gotten engaged to Lilah Fairchild. There was not a woman on the planet Mollie wanted to see Zeke pledge his eternal love to, but there wasn't a woman in the world she wanted to see him with *less* than Spring Forest native Lilah Fairchild.

Mollie was still endlessly grateful that Zeke and Lilah had broken up before that fateful walk down the aisle. Even if her unwitting role in their breakup still made her squirm when she wasn't able to push the memories from her mind.

Since Lilah, Zeke had kept his dating life separate from his life in Spring Forest. Mollie supposed he thought it easier that way, with less chance of things getting messy.

Mollie thought of the toolbox on the back porch with everything in its proper place. She reached for her glass of milk—because, of course, what else would Zeke expect her to drink?—and tried to swallow the lump in her throat. He'd stuck her in a box clearly labeled Friend, back when she was a kid, and she despaired of ever finding a way to break free.

Setting the glass back on the table, she strove for a casual tone as she said, "You hadn't mentioned going out with anyone recently."

He lifted a broad shoulder in a half shrug. "I'm not seeing anyone right now, but I could always make a call."

Because dating was that easy. Just picking up a phone and making a call. Other than Zeke, Mollie could barely remember the last conversation she'd had with the opposite sex that didn't involve her business, the shelter or estimates for something that required updating on her house.

Geez, no wonder Zeke thought he had to fix her up! Her love life really was that pathetic.

"I just thought it might make you more comfortable if I was there with you."

Mollie could think of little that would make her more uncomfortable—including stabbing hot needles into her eyes. She didn't know which would be worse—Zeke witnessing just how socially inept she was while on some painfully awkward blind date, or sitting across the table from him and watching him romance another woman.

"Right. With me. On a date."

With her but not dating her. With her while he was on a date with *another woman*.

"What about next Friday?" Zeke asked as he pulled out his phone and opened his calendar app. He knew Mollie well enough to realize she'd keep putting the date off—the way she did with the repairs around the house—unless he got her to agree to a specific day and time. "That would give me a chance to—"

"Enough!"

Surprised by the sharp comment, he glanced up from the screen. "What's wrong? Is next Friday not a good day?"

"No, Zeke," she gritted out between clenched teeth, "next Friday is not a good day."

Zeke hadn't expected her to jump at his suggestion. Not with how stubborn and independent she was. But he also hadn't expected her to stare at him like he'd lost his mind.

"Mollie—"

"There will never be a good day." Standing in front of him, she lifted her chin and glared, spots of color flaming in her cheeks. Her slender throat moved as she swallowed, and he bit back a curse.

Though he'd tried easing into the subject of setting her up, he'd clearly embarrassed her. They'd been friends for so long, sometimes he forgot how shy she could be around someone new. He'd never understood how a woman who could stare down a Rottweiler had a hard time looking a guy in the eye.

"Look, it won't be so bad."

She sucked in a deep breath. "Going on a double date with you and—" She waved a dismissive hand as she muttered, "You have no idea."

Zeke felt his own face heat at the unspoken slight against the women he dated. Not that Mollie had met any of them. No one in Spring Forest had met any of the women he'd dated since Lilah. Introducing a woman to his friends and family would be an unspoken signal that the relationship was getting serious. And Zeke didn't do serious. Not anymore.

But he'd break his own rule for Mollie. He'd do anything for Mollie.

He owed it to Patrick to look out for his little sister.

But as Mollie tossed her wild curls back and met his gaze head on, she didn't look embarrassed anymore. Sparks snapped from her blue-green eyes and her chest rose and fell as her breathing quickened. When she stepped closer and pointed a finger at him, he'd never seen her look so angry.

He'd never seen her look so *sexy.*

And Zeke wasn't thinking about his best friend or some meaningless double date with a woman from Raleigh as his blood heated in his veins. The sudden rush of desire caught him so off guard, he took a stumbling step backward when Mollie poked him in the chest.

"I don't need you to set me up. I'm doing just fine on my own."

"You—"

"I'm fine!" she repeated. "And I can get my own dates, thank you very much!"

"How am I possibly going to get my own date?" Mollie lamented to her friends Claire and Amanda the next day. The two women had answered Mollie's SOS text message, agreeing to meet her for lunch at the Main Street Grille.

With Claire's recent engagement to Matt, and as busy as Amanda was with her new catering business and with her fiancé Ryan Carter, single dad and owner/editor of the local paper, Mollie hated to drag her friends into her problems. If circumstances hadn't been so dire, she wouldn't have bothered.

But instead of seeing the problem as an insurmountable issue, Amanda and Claire exchanged eager grins.

Amanda scooted her chair closer to the table, her rich chocolate eyes bright as she said, "I've been dying for the chance to set you up."

"Huh." Wishing she could share her friend's enthusiasm, Mollie slouched in her chair and picked at her Caesar salad with her fork. "You and Zeke both."

Claire's expression turned sympathetic. "I know this isn't easy, but maybe it's time for you to move on."

Everything inside Mollie rebelled at the idea of giving up on the dream that had lived in her heart for so long. "How can you say that? Especially after the way you and Matt reunited after all these years."

"Matt and I had a history together. A romantic history, so in a way, it feels like our relationship picked up right where we left off. You and Zeke have a history, too, but it's a history of friendship."

"So you think it's hopeless, then. It is hopeless. *I'm* hopeless."

"You are far from hopeless!" Amanda argued. "You are a wonderful, amazing person who deserves a wonderful and amazing man in return."

"Zeke is—"

"A wonderful and amazing man, I know." Gentling her voice, Amanda said, "But you have to realize, hon, that he might not be the wonderful and amazing man for you."

"I've always thought he was perfect for me."

"And he is…if all you want is a friend. But if you want more than that, then it's time to admit what you and Zeke have isn't enough."

Not enough…

Mollie had spent her entire life feeling as though what she had to offer was not enough. Her brother, Patrick, had been the firstborn and everything her parents wanted in a child. Outgoing, good-looking, talented, smart—while Mollie had been little more than an afterthought.

Losing Patrick had only made Mollie long even more for a family of her own—one that consisted of at least a few two-legged members. Fostering and training dogs certainly filled a huge part of her life, but she still had an empty spot in her heart.

"I do want to get married someday, to have children," Mollie admitted.

Zeke's children...

But he wanted to pawn her off on one of his buddies. Giving up on eating, Mollie pushed her plate away. "I'm no good at dating. I never know what to say and always end up feeling so self-conscious that I don't say anything... It's just a disaster."

"All you need is a little confidence. Let us fix you up, and you'll see dating isn't so bad."

"I don't know—" Mollie was about to tell her friends to forget the whole idea when a masculine voice called out, "Hey, sis!"

The three women looked up as Amanda's older brother, Josh, walked over to their table. Like all of Amanda's siblings, Josh was blessed with warm olive skin, deep-brown eyes and dimples to die for. He greeted them with a smile before reaching over his sister's shoulder to break off a piece of her cornbread muffin. Shaking his head sadly after sampling the bite, he said, "They just aren't the same since you left."

"Stop! It's the exact same recipe," Amanda insisted, but Mollie noticed her friend had to take a taste for herself, just to make sure.

"Quit trying to guilt your sister for following her own dreams," Claire scolded him.

"Oh, come on! Giving my brothers and sisters a hard time is the best thing about having siblings." Josh caught Mollie's eye and broke off suddenly with a quiet curse. "I'm sorry, Mollie, I wasn't thinking—Patrick was a true hero."

"Yes, he was," Mollie murmured around the ache in her throat, as she always did when anyone brought up her brother and his service. Like everyone else in Spring Forest, she was proud of and humbled by her brother's dedication and bravery.

Patrick had been an amazing man and a remarkable soldier. But the brother she mourned, the brother she missed, had also been human. He'd had his fears, his doubts, and he'd made mistakes.

But her parents, Zeke, the whole town wanted to remember Patrick McFadden as the heroic soldier who had died for his country. For all of them, and for the sake of her brother's memory, Mollie would do everything in her power to keep it that way.

She held on to her smile despite the sting of tears as she added, "He would be the first to agree with you about how much he enjoyed giving me a hard time."

Looking slightly relieved at her joke, Josh grinned. "Patrick loved to kid around, but every guy in Spring Forest knew not to mess with you or they'd have a pissed-off soldier on their hands."

Looking as puzzled as Mollie felt, Amanda asked, "What do you mean, Josh?"

His dark brows rose. "You didn't know? Before he left for basic training, Patrick had a heart-to-heart with every teenaged dude in the county, making sure they all knew his little sis was off-limits."

Noticing the look her friends exchanged, Mollie reached for her iced tea, half surprised she didn't spill it down the front of her shirt as she took a quick sip. "That's ridiculous," she muttered into the glass. "I was a kid when he left."

"You were fourteen," Amanda pointed out.

Josh nodded. "And Patrick already knew what the rest of us figured out in high school—that you'd turn into a beautiful young woman." Josh shot her a quick wink that had Mollie's face flaming. "He was right to warn us all away."

After Josh excused himself and headed to the kitchen to speak with his brother-in-law, typical sounds still filled the restaurant—the clink of silverware against plates, the waitresses taking orders, the din of conversation all around. But a dead silence had fallen over their table.

"Well, there you have it," Claire announced finally.

Amanda nodded. "The reason you've had such a hard time dating all these years had nothing to do with you. After Patrick warned them off, guys got used to thinking of you as off-limits, and that never changed."

Was it possible? Mollie thought back to her high school days, when it seemed every girl had a date for Homecoming, Spring Fling, Prom…every girl but her. Mollie had believed she was somehow at fault. She was too shy, too awkward, too plain. Was it her big brother's warning that had really kept the boys away?

"Why would he do that?"

"You know how Patrick wanted to protect you." Amanda reached out to squeeze Mollie's hand. "He was gone so much, he didn't have the chance to see the strong, confident, beautiful woman you've become."

"Now it's time for the rest of Spring Forest to take notice," Claire added.

The idea of anyone noticing her had Mollie ready to

break out in hives, and Claire and Amanda wanted the *whole town* to take note? "I don't know—"

"You heard what Josh said and—" Amanda's eyes flew open wide. "Oh, my gosh! I can't believe I didn't think of this before, but Josh would be perfect for you!"

"Josh? But he's—"

"He's what?" her friend asked a little defensively. "Yes, he's my pain-in-the-neck brother, but he's also smart, funny, good-looking. Give me one good reason why you don't want to go out with him."

Mollie didn't bother to give the only reason that truly mattered…

He wasn't Zeke.

Mollie smiled with a touch of pride as she gazed at the gorgeous guy across the table. "Congratulations, Stanley! You have officially graduated!" Though she knew the six-pound papillon didn't understand, she couldn't help thinking the tiny dog was grinning as he sat in his mistress's lap.

"My good, good boy!" If Stanley was grinning, his owner, Mrs. Winchester, was positively glowing. The wealthy sixtysomething widow wore a stylish pale pink pantsuit. Gold and diamonds flashed at her slender wrists as she lifted Stanley toward her face.

Mrs. W, as she preferred to be called, had an active social life that included playing bridge, meeting friends for lunch and going on long shopping excursions. All of which she wanted to do with Stanley trotting by her side or riding in his custom-made carrier. But the tiny dog's guarding behavior had made that a challenge.

As part of a "final exam," Mollie and Mrs. W had met for brunch at a trendy restaurant in downtown Raleigh. The summer day was slightly overcast and cool, perfect for dining alfresco on the dog-friendly patio. "He's been a perfect gentleman, if I do say so myself." The dog hadn't growled or snapped once. "And he certainly looks the part."

In honor of the occasion, Mrs. W had dressed her boy in a tuxedo, complete with bow tie, top hat and tails. Not that Mollie was judging. She'd been known to dress Arti up for certain holidays. Her favorite costume included a single antler tied to the dog's head, à la Max from the classic Christmas cartoon.

At the end of the meal, Mrs. W gave Mollie a perfumed hug with Stanley sandwiched between them. "I can't thank you enough, Mollie. I do enjoy going out, and I hate the idea of leaving poor Stanley home all alone in that big house by himself."

Mrs. W's husband, the original Stanley, had left her with a significant fortune and the mansion to match. Mollie had a feeling that the elderly woman was the one who truly felt too alone.

And while she might not have the fortune or the mansion, Mollie certainly understood the companionship of a four-legged friend. With a final reassurance that the woman could always call if Stanley regressed at any point, Mollie said goodbye to her client. With her next lesson not scheduled until later that afternoon, Mollie decided to stroll along the outdoor mall.

She wasn't much of a shopper, but she found herself lingering in front of a brightly lit boutique. She didn't know how she'd escaped lunch the other day without promising Amanda she could set her up with Josh. If she agreed, and that was a big if, she should probably think about buying something new to wear.

Faceless mannequins flaunted skinny arms and legs, their slender forms draped in an array of short-skirted, low-cut, skintight dresses. Signs and posters promoted red-hot looks and sizzling summer sales. For a split second she considered stepping inside, but no… This was why she didn't go shopping. Or go out, for that matter.

Mollie sighed as she moved to the next shop, this one worse than the last. Bright white lettering and a sleek black background provided a stark contrast to the hot pink awning. The storefront offered a lavish display of lacy lingerie. Matching bras and panties—some satin, some sheer. Baby-doll nighties, silk kimono-style peignoirs. In every shade of the rainbow, plus a few animal prints thrown in to appease a woman's—*or man's*—wild side.

Despite her career choice, Mollie feared she did not have a wild side. Her own underwear, like the rest of her wardrobe, was selected for function rather than fashion, with nothing satin, sheer or sexy about it. With the late morning sun shining behind her, she could see herself in the glass. Button-down khaki camp shirt. Olive green capri pants. Hair caught back in a ponytail.

Red-hot? Sizzling? More like bland and boring.

But if she stood just right, she could see the shimmery reflection of an emerald nightie draped over her body. The image was as transparent as the sheer material of the lace-trimmed gown, but she could almost feel the cool, silken whisper against her skin…

"Hey, Mollie! I thought that was you."

Mollie…it's always been you…

So lost in the moment, feeling almost trapped within the glass, her heart leaped to her throat when she realized the sight of Zeke standing behind her was not part of her fantasy. Wearing a maroon dress shirt open at his strong throat, sleeves rolled back over his leanly muscled forearms, and a pair of slate-gray trousers, Zeke Harper in the flesh was far sexier than any desire-filled daydream.

Turning around quickly enough to make her head spin, she tried to grab hold of the longing inside her that was getting harder and harder to ignore. Zeke's practice was only a few blocks away, but Mollie hadn't expected to run into him. She hadn't exactly been avoiding him, but at the same time, she wasn't sure she was ready to face him, either.

You have to realize he might not be the man for you.

Her head was starting to get the picture, but her heart insisted on coloring outside the lines. She soaked in the sight of him, not wanting to admit how much she'd missed him. The cool breeze ruffled his hair just the way Mollie longed to do, and the way the fine linen molded to his chest was sexy enough to make her mouth go bone dry.

"What are you doing here?" he asked with an easy smile that faded into a frown when he stared at the store behind her.

Her entire body flushed hot, as if he'd caught her wearing one of the revealing negligees. Hadn't she imagined the feel of emerald silk or black satin against her skin while gazing through the glass? Was it possible that Zeke—

Mollie dismissed the thought. If not for his recent "encouragement" for her to start dating, she would have sworn Zeke didn't know she was a woman at all.

"I met a client for brunch." Unable to stop herself, she added, "And then thought I'd do some shopping."

"Shopping?" He echoed the word as if he'd never heard her say it before—which, Mollie admitted, was entirely possible. The doors behind them swished open as a satisfied, or perhaps soon-to-be satisfied, customer stepped outside, hot pink bags in hand. The fragrance of warm vanilla drifted out from the store along with the soft, seductive strains of a love song.

But it was standing so close to Zeke that had Mollie's senses reeling. Breathing in his spicy cologne mixed with the soft, feminine scent left her light-headed, and she couldn't think of trying on the seductive lingerie without imagining Zeke taking it off.

Staring up into his hazel eyes, for a split second she thought she saw all the heat, all the desire, all the want she longed to see shimmering in their endless depths. She'd always loved his eyes, so rich and warm with the intriguing, ever-changing kaleidoscope of gold and green... She stood close enough to see herself reflected there, like her image in the glass, and in a sudden, painful rush, she knew.

All the heat, desire, want she saw shining in his eyes was her own.

And oh, God...

What if Zeke could see it, too?

Because the only thing more completely humiliating than a hopeless crush on her best friend would be her best friend knowing about it!

She stumbled back a few steps, nearly falling into a nearby trash can before catching her balance. "Yes, shopping! For a new chew toy. For the dogs," she blurted out, just in case Zeke actually thought the chew toy was for her. Her cheeks burning in helpless mortification, she waved a hand down the line of shops. "There's a pet store around the corner."

"Oh, right." Shaking his head, Zeke gave a small laugh that held a slight hint of relief. "Pet store. How are the new dogs?"

Grateful to focus on something else, Mollie said,

"Charlie's settling in." She'd introduced the two foster dogs to Arti, and as she'd expected, her goofy hound dog had greeted them with eager sniffs, happy to have some new playmates. She definitely didn't have to worry about the two girls...

Almost as if reading her mind, Zeke asked, "And Chief?"

"He's...coming along." In the few days since bringing Chief home from the shelter, Mollie had witnessed how truly traumatized the poor dog was. The large backyard both Charlie and Arti loved was too big and intimidating for the frightened shepherd. "It's going to take time, but I feel like I had a breakthrough yesterday using a tethering technique with Charlie."

"Tethering?"

Nodding, Mollie explained how she'd used a carabiner to hook the end of Charlie's leash to Chief's collar, connecting the two dogs. "Charlie isn't afraid of anything, and it doesn't take much to get her to run around the yard." With a soft laugh, she added, "Poor Chief didn't have any choice but to follow."

The objects that were too scary for the shepherd to face on his own had been so much easier to handle with Charlie leading the way. Mollie had watched in satisfaction as the Lab wandered off with Chief happily trailing behind.

"That's great, Mollie." Pride filled Zeke's expression as he smiled down at her, and it was easy to forget how frustrating he could be sometimes. "Sounds like you're making real progress."

"Yeah." With Chief. Too bad she couldn't say the same for herself. Standing so close to Zeke, basking in his praise, it was easy to forget the realization she'd had working with the dogs.

On a professional level, Mollie appreciated the tethering technique. But on a far more personal level, as she'd watched the two dogs together, she couldn't avoid the obvious comparison.

As the kid sister, she'd always been the one tagging along, following her beloved big brother and his best friend. But Patrick was no longer there for her to follow, and Zeke—

Zeke would never see her for the woman she was as long as she was still walking in the same steps as the girl she'd always been.

"I'm meeting some colleagues for lunch," he was saying. After glancing at his watch, he offered, "You want to come?"

Tagging along...

Mollie shook her head. "I still have my shopping to do."

"Ah, yes. Your chew toy. For the dogs." His lips lifted in a teasing smile, one Mollie was suddenly determined to wipe from his gorgeous face.

She needed to prove she was woman enough to choose her own path. And if he didn't see that—if he *couldn't* see that—well, then, maybe it was time for Mollie to turn her attention to a man who did.

"That's right, and something for me."

Spinning around, she stepped toward the lingerie store. In the split second before the automatic doors to the vanilla-and-spice-scented shop opened, she caught a satisfying glimpse of Zeke's stunned expression in the reflective glass.

Chapter Four

"Hey, sorry I'm late."

Zeke looked up from his coffee as his friend Matt Fielding claimed the seat across from him. "No worries." He lifted his cup in greeting. "I just ordered."

The two men typically met at Whole Bean Coffee Saturday mornings before heading over to the local gym to shoot hoops. Matt was still working his way back from injuries sustained while he was in the army but insisted the games of b-ball were far less stressful on his leg than the rigors of physical therapy.

"How's everything going?" he asked over the din of caffeine-laced conversation going on all around them.

As usual, the coffee shop was crowded. He'd spotted Mollie's friend Amanda and the new shelter director, Rebekah Taylor, earlier, but Mollie wasn't with them. Not that Zeke expected her to be. Her weekends were usually booked solid with the group classes she offered. Most evenings she gave private lessons to dogs and owners who either preferred one-on-one meetings or needed more individual help.

Add in the two new foster dogs and the additional work she'd taken on since the tornado had hit the shelter, and she certainly had her hands full.

No doubt that was the reason she hadn't returned his calls or texts for the past few days.

"And then Ellie and Sparkle decided to run off and join the circus."

"That's great, Matt, and—wait, what did you say?"

"Does it matter?" his friend asked wryly. "Since you haven't been listening since I sat down."

"Sorry, I was thinking about Mollie."

Matt's eyebrows rose. "Really?"

"Yeah." Zeke sighed. "I'm worried about her. Seems like all she does is work with her dogs."

"Some people could say the same about you and your patients, not to mention all the time you spend at the veteran support group."

For Zeke, volunteering was the least he could do to try to repay the soldiers who had sacrificed so much. Soldiers like Patrick... In the months after his friend's death, Zeke had reached out to the local VA and organized a therapy group for former soldiers to come and share their experiences. But no matter how many hours he spent helping the wounded warriors who had returned home, the time had yet to ease his own feelings of loss.

Of guilt.

"I've been home for months, and you haven't mentioned seeing anyone special."

Giving his head a quick shake, Zeke reached for his coffee and took a large swallow of the strong brew.

"Maybe it has been a while," he told his friend. Zeke realized he couldn't remember the last woman he'd gone out with. Not that Matt would have known about his dates either way.

Ever since his broken engagement, Zeke had kept his dating life separate from his friends and family. Oh, sure, someday if he met a woman and things got serious, he'd have to cross that line, but he didn't see that happening. Not for a long, long time.

Not after Lilah…

Lilah had moved to town right before his senior year, and the elder Fairchilds and Harpers became quick friends. Much to his teenaged mortification, his parents asked him to show Lilah, the new girl, around. They hadn't understood how ridiculous the request was. In a small town like Spring Forest, the blonde, beautiful newcomer was instantly the most popular girl in school.

All the boys, including Zeke, were smitten. But even as a geeky teen, he'd known he didn't stand a chance. Lilah had a type, and he didn't fit the star quarterback, homecoming king, cool kid mold. She and Patrick had even briefly dated the summer before his friend went off to boot camp.

She'd left after graduation, but a few years ago she'd stunned the town by moving back home. At the time, Zeke hadn't given it much thought. He'd grown up. He'd moved on. Lilah—and his ridiculous crush—were part of his past. Or so he thought, until he'd gone out with his coworkers and spotted her at the hottest new nightclub in Raleigh. In all the years they'd known each other, she'd never given him a second look. But that night, he'd felt the full-on impact across the crowded bar as she'd checked him out head to toe…

And with one look, he'd been hooked.

Their parents had been thrilled when he and Lilah started dating and absolutely ecstatic when they got engaged. Friends for over a decade, they'd celebrated the idea of becoming family... But when the engagement ended, so too did that friendship.

"I offered to fix Mollie up," he told Matt.

"You?" Choking on a sip of coffee, Matt set his mug aside. "Sorry if I don't see you in the role of cupid."

Zeke waved the image of the arrow-shooting cherub aside. "I know Mollie better than anyone, and I'm good at reading people. I thought I could find the right kind of guy for her."

"I'm, wow, really not sure where to start with any of that, but okay, Mr. People Reader. Who's the guy?"

When Zeke had first mentioned the idea to Mollie, at least a dozen single guys had come to mind, but since then... Since then, he'd watched Mollie walk into a shop filled with sexy lingerie and he hadn't been able to get the image of her draped in satin and silk and lace out of his mind.

If mixing his dating life with his friends and family was a line in the sand he wouldn't cross, then even considering any kind of romantic relationship with Mollie was the Great Wall of China. He and Patrick had long ago sworn they were brothers in every way that mattered, which made Mollie like a sister to him, and he would not—could not—think of her in any other way.

But there was nothing to stop any guy she went out with from imagining all that and more...and he really had to ask himself why he thought Mollie dating was such a good idea in the first place.

"I'm—I'm not sure," he muttered. "It can't be just anyone."

"Well, what about Dan Sutton?"

The local lawyer was well respected in Spring Forest despite the fair share of gossip surrounding the disintegration of his business partnership and marriage after his partner and his wife ran off together. Still, Zeke shook his head. "He has his hands full raising his three girls."

"I don't know," Matt argued. "Maybe as a single dad he's looking for someone to help lighten the load. And look how Dillon helped bring Ryan and Amanda together."

Dillon was Ryan's six-year-old son, and what had started out as a pretend engagement to appease the boy's grandparents had quickly turned into a genuine love match.

"Dan's a good guy, but he's not right for Mollie. He's a bit too conservative." Zeke couldn't see the man putting up with a layer of dog hair all over his expensive suits. "Mollie needs someone more down-to-earth."

"What about Cade Battle then? You can't get much more down-to-earth than a farmer," Matt pointed out, but Zeke was already shaking his head.

"Cade's too much of a loner." Though the hardworking man had a soft spot for the Whitaker sisters and partnered with them to foster some of the less domesticated animals that showed up at the shelter, he barely gave the time of day to anyone else.

Matt brought up a few more guys—Grant Whitaker, the Whitaker sisters' nephew, and Davis Macintyre, a vet tech at the shelter, but Zeke shook his head. "Grant is heading back to Florida after the renovations on the shelter are complete. And Davis is even more introverted than Mollie. She needs someone who can help bring her out of her shell a little."

"The way you do," Matt pointed out.

"Exactly! I mean, not *me* exactly. Mollie's comfortable around me because we've been friends for so long." And friends certainly did *not* picture friends wearing nothing but barely there lingerie.

"And you're sure that's all there is to it?"

"Of course it is." Friendship was all there could be. "I've known her since she was in braces and pigtails," he said, as much to remind himself as his friend.

Matt offered Zeke a sidelong glance. "So you think, just because you've known someone for years, you've already discovered all there is to them?"

Okay, maybe he didn't know *everything*, but he knew Mollie better than anyone. But even after Matt named several more single guys they both knew, Zeke couldn't picture any of them with Mollie. Whenever he tried… something inside him rebelled at the thought.

"Seems to me like no one around here is good enough for Mollie," Matt finally determined.

Zeke couldn't help breathing a sigh of relief that they had drawn a blank. But he wasn't about to admit that to Matt. "I'm sure there's someone I'm not thinking of."

"Yep," his friend murmured into his cup. "Pretty sure there is."

Needing a change in subject, Zeke asked, "How's the new job treating you?"

After moving back to Spring Forest, Matt had taken a job with Bobby Doyle at his auto shop. A field mechanic during his years in the service, Matt had always had a way with machines, and the two veterans had hit it off from the start.

"The job's great."

"But?" Zeke prompted when his friend's frown contradicted his words.

"I'm still worried about Bobby, man. I've seen him experience several flashbacks, even though he won't admit it, and I know he's dealing with PTSD."

"I take it you still haven't had any luck convincing him to come to one of the support groups," Zeke surmised.

PTSD wasn't the only issue facing former soldiers. Some dealt with anxiety, depression, survivor's remorse. Some turned to alcohol or drugs to dull their pain, but Zeke did his best to get the word out about the therapy groups. To let veterans like Bobby know help was available.

But Matt was already shaking his head. "I've asked him to come a few times, but he always shoots me down. Bobby's a whiz around cars—any kind of machine, really. He's the guy people call when they need something fixed. I don't think he's ready to admit this is something he can't fix on his own."

Frustration and concern filled Matt's voice. Returning to civilian life wasn't easy for many veterans, and the mental scars of serving tours overseas didn't stay overseas when the soldiers came home. "There's gotta be something more I can do."

The feeling was one Zeke knew well. How many times since Patrick's death had he questioned what more he could have done to help his friend? During that last visit home, he'd sensed Patrick was struggling. More than once, he'd tried to get his friend to open up about whatever was bothering him.

But when Patrick had flatly stated that he wanted to hang out on his friend's sofa, not on a shrink's couch, Zeke backed off. He'd trusted Patrick when he said he simply needed to decompress and that when the time was right, they would talk.

But that right time never came. And though he and Patrick had hung out several times during that visit, playing a few games of hoops, shooting rounds of pool, sharing some beers while watching the college basketball championships, they never did have that talk.

Patrick had taken his secrets with him when he left Spring Forest, and Zeke couldn't help wondering if those secrets and the weight his friend carried with him had been a factor in his death.

If Zeke had found a way, if he'd tried harder to convince Patrick to confide in him, would his best friend still be alive?

"Are you ready for this?" Amanda and Claire exchanged excited grins as the three women stood in Mollie's bedroom, prepared for the big unveiling.

After spending what felt like endless hours being tugged and teased, spritzed and sprayed within an inch of her life, Mollie's head was pounding. Her feet, crammed into a borrowed pair of too-small shoes, ached, and she was pretty sure she'd either bust a seam or possibly break a rib if she took too big a breath while wearing the dress she'd pulled out from the back of her closet.

Throughout the entire makeover, her friends had kept Mollie from catching even the smallest peek in a mirror. As much as she appreciated their efforts, she worried the end result would only be a disappointment. Even though the two women had brought over enough beauty products and styling tools to open their own salon, her own "plain Jane" look was bound to show through.

"You know this is crazy, right? I mean, there isn't enough makeup in the world to cover up who I really am."

"No one is trying to cover you up, Mollie!" Amanda insisted. "You are an amazing, wonderful, *beautiful* woman."

"We want to highlight that, not disguise it," Claire agreed.

"And you really think bright red lipstick and a bee-hive hairdo is gonna do that?" she asked dubiously.

Mollie had never been a hair and makeup kind of girl, despite—or perhaps because of—her mother's "encouragement."

Honestly, Mollie, are you really going out of the house looking like that? *You could at least* try *to cover those freckles, and would it kill you to do* something *with that hair?*

At a time when most preteen girls were dying to experiment with eyeliner, mascara and the newest celebrity hairstyle, Mollie had clung to her tomboy ways. A decade or so later, nothing had changed. Not her freckles, not her curly hair…and not her mother's disappointment in her only daughter.

"Okay, first, that is Color Me Roses red, and this is not the nineteen-sixties. Your hair is in an elegant, *timeless* chignon, not a beehive."

"Which you would know," Claire chimed in with a hint of laughter in her voice, "if you actually turned around to look in the mirror."

Realizing she was stalling, Mollie heaved a sigh, turned on her uncomfortable borrowed heels and stared at the woman staring back at her…

"Oh, my fairy godmother. I look—"

"Amazing!" Amanda interjected, but for Mollie that didn't even begin to describe the transformation.

Gone were the flyaway reddish-blond curls that normally shielded her face. Instead, her hair was smoothly pulled back at the nape of her neck in an elegant twist. Makeup lightly highlighted her freckles and gave her skin a warm glow. Her fair lashes looked almost ridiculously long and lush, surrounding eyes that could only be described as smoky.

Add in the sleeveless, emerald silk wraparound dress—one her mother had insisted she buy for her cousin's wedding last year—and Mollie hardly recognized herself.

Anticipation shot a dozen or so sparklers off in her stomach, and she clasped her hands at her waist, holding her head a little higher, her shoulders a little straighter. She couldn't believe how confident and sophisticated she looked. How confident and sophisticated she felt.

Not like Patrick's tagalong little sister. Not like Zeke's best buddy. But like the kind of woman who would turn a guy's head and keep him looking long after she'd walked by. Like the kind of woman a man would truly notice for the first time...

"Josh isn't going to know what hit him!"

Josh...

Mollie gave a sudden start, hit by a mix of disappointment and guilt. Zeke wasn't going to notice her at all because she wasn't going out with Zeke. All this effort was supposed to be for Josh, but Mollie hadn't given her date more than a moment's thought since her friends arrived.

When Josh had called Mollie to confirm their date,

he'd been outgoing and charming, every bit the catch his sister vowed he was.

But he's not Zeke.

Shaking off the reminder, Mollie turned to give each of her friends a hug. "Thank you both for this. You've pulled off the miracle you promised."

"No miracle. Remember, Josh already thinks you're beautiful." Amanda turned Mollie back to the mirror. "All of this is about making you believe it."

Mollie tried keeping her friend's words in mind once Amanda and Claire left and the doubts started to creep in. Josh was taking her to a restaurant in Raleigh. What if she ran out of things to say within the first few minutes and had to sit in the passenger seat in painful silence for the half-hour ride? What if the restaurant was some super-fancy place where she wouldn't recognize any of the offerings on the menu? What if—

A knock on the front door interrupted her panic. Along with being outgoing and charming and handsome, Josh was also punctual.

But when she opened the door, the man waiting on the other side, highlighted by the fading summer sunlight, was not her date. Instead it was the man she'd so hopelessly fallen in love with.

Chapter Five

Zeke stared at the woman in front of him. Blinked his eyes hard. Stared some more.

If he didn't know the road to Mollie's house as well as he knew his own, if he didn't recognize the door he'd spent a day last fall stripping, sanding and painting a bright red, if he hadn't stood on this porch hundreds of times over the past few years, Zeke might have believed he'd somehow shown up at a stranger's house.

Because the woman standing in front of him—her hair caught back in some fancy twist, her lips stained a lush red, her body sheathed in a silky green dress that hugged all her curves—couldn't possibly be Mollie.

Not his Mollie—the girl he'd saved from the fast-running creek that ran behind their childhood homes when she'd jumped in to rescue the dog she'd later named Shadow. The skinny tomboy who'd tagged along after him and Patrick every chance she could. The shy dog trainer who never wore anything but jeans and a T-shirt with her hair in a ponytail and nothing more than sunscreen on her face.

That was his Mollie. This—this was a woman he didn't recognize.

"Zeke," the not-Mollie said, a hint of natural color shining through behind the blush on her cheeks. "What are you doing here?"

"I'm, um—" After his conversation with Matt and seeing some of the veterans with their service dogs at the center, Zeke had wondered if that might be the answer for Bobby Doyle. At first, he'd been disappointed to learn about the long wait lists and the years of instruction required for a dog to act as a disabled vet's eyes or arms or legs. But Bobby wasn't physically disabled. His needs were different, and perhaps less training would be necessary.

And who would know more about training than Mollie?

Plus, he'd needed an excuse to see her. Which was weird considering he'd never needed one before. Then again, Mollie had never ignored his calls and texts before.

Not his Mollie...

But his plan to help Bobby was the last thing on his mind as he gaped, slack-jawed, at the woman in front of him. "What are you *wearing*?"

And where on earth did she think she was going dressed like that?

"I'm—um." Mollie glanced down, seeming almost as surprised as he was by the bare arms, the hint of creamy cleavage and shapely calves on display. As short as she was, Zeke had never imagined her legs could be so long. Hell, until the other day in her backyard, he'd never imagined her legs at all, yet now he couldn't help but wonder how he'd gone so long *not* noticing.

He had to jerk his gaze upward when Mollie started speaking, suddenly unable to do two things at once—not as long as one of those things was staring at Mollie's legs.

"...my cousin's wedding last year," she was saying, but looking at her face wasn't doing his concentration any favors.

Not when the last rays of sunlight glinted off her hair, turning every strand a fiery reddish-gold. Not when her lips were painted a bright crimson that should have clashed and yet didn't. And certainly not when Charlie tried to nose her way through the open door, and Mollie bent to catch the dog's collar. As she reached down, the bodice's V-neckline gaped, offering a view of gently rounded female flesh that a true gentleman would have ignored, but no real man could resist.

And Zeke had never doubted that he was a red-blooded male with a healthy appreciation for beautiful women. Except this wasn't just any woman. This was Mollie, his friend! One of his best friends. And she wasn't supposed to be beautiful. She was supposed to be—Mollie. Cute, sure. Sweet, too. But not...

Sexy.

The description came out of nowhere, but try as he might, Zeke couldn't deny it.

"Wait...if your cousin's wedding was last year, why are you wearing that dress now?"

Mollie frowned as she stepped back into the living room. "Honestly, Zeke, are you feeling okay? You are acting really weird. Do you need a drink or something?"

He must have managed to nod because Mollie turned

and led the way into her kitchen. Following along behind her, Zeke couldn't shake the uneasy sensation turning him inside out. Everything was the same as Mollie moved about the small space, reaching for a glass in the overhead cupboards and pouring him a glass of orange juice that she kept around only because he liked it. But as she handed him the drink and their fingers brushed around the cool glass, Zeke knew.

Everything had changed.

He downed the juice in one continuous swallow, as if low blood sugar had anything do with the sudden rush of desire pulsing through him at the simple, innocent touch. Mollie was still eyeing him closely when he finished.

As he set the glass on the counter, she explained, "You asked what I was wearing. This is a dress I bought for my cousin's wedding last year. I'm wearing it tonight because I'm going…out." That natural blush was back, and Mollie avoided his gaze as she grabbed the glass and carried it over to the sink.

"What do you mean, out?"

Turning to face him, she huffed out a sigh. "You know, as in going out on a date. Or you certainly should know, considering this was all your idea in the first place!"

"My idea?" Zeke was a hundred percent certain he'd never had any idea that Mollie could look so… Jerking his thoughts away from the forbidden direction they kept taking, he asked, "How was this my idea?"

Her eyes narrowed in an annoyed expression he recognized despite the layers of makeup and inch-long lashes. "You were the one who said I need to get out more, remember?"

He had said that, hadn't he? "But not with just anyone! I was going to set you up. With the right guy," he stressed, which only earned him another withering look.

"How do you know Josh isn't the right guy?"

"Josh?"

Mollie nodded. "Josh Sylvester, Amanda's brother."

Though Zeke didn't know the other man well, he remembered Josh from high school and knew he had recently moved back to town take a job as the athletic director at Spring Forest High. Josh was friendly, outgoing and in great shape, thanks to his job. Zeke supposed most women would consider him handsome. That Mollie was going out with a Spring Forest local rather than some stranger should have made Zeke feel better.

It didn't.

"How do you know he's not the right guy?" she repeated.

"Because I know you, Mollie." But he didn't know what it was about that statement that had her rolling her eyes. Or what it was about the whole conversation that was making his heart and his head start to pound. "That's why I wanted to be the one to fix you up."

"Well, now you don't have to. You can check that off your list of Things about Mollie that Need Fixing."

Stung by her sarcasm, he argued, "I never said anything about you needed to be fixed."

He held her gaze until her shoulders lowered ever so slightly and she lost the defensive lift to her chin. "Maybe you didn't say it, and I know you're just trying to be a good friend, but I don't need your help, Zeke."

Because she didn't need him? Zeke sucked in a breath, startled by the swift pain in his chest at the thought.

"I'm a big girl now," Mollie was saying. "All grown-up and able to make my own decisions." She wrinkled her nose in a way that took him right back to the days when she hadn't been so grown-up. "And choose my own dates."

"I know," he agreed. Logically, he knew full well that Mollie was a capable, intelligent woman. But she still was—and always would be—Patrick's little sister. And he owed it to his friend to look out for her. He'd made a promise, and this was one he planned to keep. "I'm just trying to protect you."

"From Josh?" Incredulity filled her voice. "He's the brother of one of my best friends! I know him almost as well as I know you."

The comment shouldn't have hurt as much as it did. He and Mollie were more than friends. They were *best* friends and had been for years. Whatever she knew—or *thought* she knew—about Josh Sylvester couldn't possibly compare! "And Josh?" he challenged as he stepped closer. "Does he know you as well as I do?"

The look she shot him, a look he didn't recognize and couldn't begin to read, gave the answer before Mollie did. "Honestly, Zeke, sometimes I don't think you know me at all."

Josh Sylvester was every bit as smart and funny and charming as his sister had advertised. On the ride to the restaurant, he kept her laughing with stories about growing up in the family restaurant.

"Of course, after Amanda jumped ship, the folks hoped I would somehow step into her shoes."

"Any chance of that happening?"

"Not if they want to stay in business. The Sylvester talent for cooking skipped right over me. The Sylvester talent for eating, however, is alive and well." Josh's grin flashed in the passing streetlights as he glanced over at her. "I thought we'd try the new seafood restaurant over in Raleigh. It got a great write-up in the *Chronicle*," he said, referring to Spring Forest's paper, run by Ryan Carter, Amanda's fiancé. "Unless…you don't like seafood?"

Realizing he'd picked up on her silence, Mollie rushed to insist, "No, I do. I love seafood." So, too, did Zeke, and she'd been holding off on trying the new restaurant until the two of them could go together.

Mollie didn't want to think about Zeke, but the uncomfortable way their last conversation ended had been playing in the back of her mind. Perhaps she had overreacted, but his response to her finding a date of her own was too similar to the way her parents had treated her while she was growing up… Offering their approval only so long as Mollie followed their rules and did things their way. Needless to say, living in a fixer-upper on the outskirts of town with a pack of dogs was *not* the McFadden way.

Patrick had been the first to support her, encouraging her to use the money she'd received in their grandmother's will to buy her own place and establish Best Friends. So had Zeke…

Because I know you, Mollie.

He thought he knew her so well that he could find the perfect man for her? Then how was it he missed seeing that guy staring back at him every morning when he looked in the mirror?

Honestly, she didn't know how she stopped herself from clobbering him over the head with one of her pointy, uncomfortable shoes!

Wiggling her pinched toes inside of those shoes,

Mollie held back a sigh. All that effort. She would have thought Zeke might have at least said *something* about her makeover.

Josh did, her conscience goaded her, adding to the pinpricks of guilt for wishing the words had come from another man. Her date, who had arrived only minutes after Zeke left, had presented her with a bouquet of flowers and told her she looked amazing.

And he'd clearly invested a bit of effort himself. Instead of the typical jeans and T-shirt she was used to seeing him in around town, tonight he wore a pair of slate-gray slacks and a pale green button-down shirt.

"You know, I was really glad when Amanda brought up the idea of the two of us going out," Josh said once they'd arrived at the elegant restaurant with its glowing lanterns and river-stone facade.

"You were?"

Josh chuckled at her surprise. "I like biking and hiking on the trails around town," he said as he placed a hand on the small of her back and led her toward the carved double doors. "I figure with your dog training we might have similar interests."

"You're right." Some of her favorite moments were the quiet times she spent outdoors, hitting the trails with Arti. Of course, more often than not, Zeke was with her on those hikes, so little wonder she took such pleasure in them.

Determined to shove the other man from her thoughts, Mollie focused on her date as the hostess seated them in a secluded corner of the restaurant. The crystal water glasses sparkled in the flickering candlelight, adding to the romantic ambience. Josh held out the chair for her, and Mollie smiled at the gentlemanly gesture.

As they discussed some of their favorite trails, Josh's grin broadened. "I have a feeling if we went hiking together, you'd leave me in the dust."

"We'll have to see, won't we?" she suggested, a little surprised by the flirtatious tone in her own voice.

Josh chuckled. "It's a date."

A second date, Mollie thought, a little amazed. Maybe this whole going-out thing wasn't as hard as she'd thought.

The waitress stopped by to take their orders, and Mollie chose the blackened salmon with a side of hasselback potatoes while Josh selected the ahi tuna and roasted asparagus along with a bottle of Viognier. Though not much of a drinker, Mollie loved the mix of crisp and fruity flavors from the first sip to the last swallow as she finished off her second glass at the end of the night.

"What do you think?" Josh asked as the waitress came by with a platter loaded with a variety of decadent desserts—key lime pie, crème brûlée, cherry cheesecake, molten lava cake. "Did you save room for the best part of the meal?"

Mollie laughed. "I'm stuffed!" The flaky fish had been cooked to perfection with a blend of Cajun spices and the buttery potatoes had practically melted in her mouth.

"You know Amanda's going to want a full report." At Mollie's startled look, he explained, "On our dinner…including what we had for dessert."

"Oh, right." She was pretty sure her friend would be disappointed if Mollie cut the night short. "I'm going to go to the ladies' room. Why don't you pick something and we can share?"

At Josh's nod, Mollie pushed back from the table and

made her way to the restrooms. She thought she might actually be getting the hang of high heels, as she only stumbled once.

As she washed her hands, she took a moment to check out her reflection in the gilded mirror hanging above the gold-flecked marble vanity. Somehow, the magic her friends had worked had lasted throughout the evening. Her hair was still swept back in the elegant twist and her makeup was still in place. She had barely exhaled a sigh of relief when the restroom's frosted glass door swung open.

"If it isn't Mousy Mollie McFadden."

Mollie froze at the sound of the familiar voice—one that had tormented her during her freshman year of high school and then come back to haunt her in far more painful fashion years later. She jerked her hands back as the water suddenly turned scalding, and met Lilah Fairchild's smirk in the mirror.

"Lilah… What are you doing here?"

The stunning blonde tossed her straight waist-length hair over a bare shoulder as she sashayed toward the second mirror. "Doing here instead of in Paris, you mean?"

The City of Lights was not exactly where Mollie had been picturing the other woman for the past two years, but she managed to mumble, "Yeah, sure."

"I moved back a few months ago." Her brows rose in fake surprise. "Didn't Zeke tell you?"

Mollie's fist clutched at the paper towel she'd pulled from the dispenser. Lilah loved pushing buttons, and much to Mollie's mortification, the other woman had known for well over a decade how completely her feelings for Zeke tied her heart into knots. Unwilling to allow Lilah to get the best of her, Mollie finished dry-ing her hands and tossed the wet towel into the trash before answering. "Actually, he didn't. You must have completely slipped his mind."

Lilah's dark eyes narrowed. "Well, then, I guess I'll just have to remind him, won't I? Is he here with you tonight?" Lowering her voice to a supposedly confidential whisper, she asked, "Has he finally given in to that pity…date you've been longing for all these years?"

Though Mollie had spent most of the night wishing she'd been with Zeke—despite Josh's perfectly charming company—she was glad he was miles away and safe in Spring Forest. "I'm here with someone else."

Lilah smirked. "It's about time you got over that pathetic crush of yours. Of course, if Zeke isn't seeing anyone, I might just have to look him up."

"Like you'd let something like that stop you," Mollie muttered beneath her breath as the other woman strolled out of the restroom in a catwalk-like turn of blond hair and expensive perfume.

The dinner that had been so delicious a few minutes ago threatened to make a not-so-appetizing reappearance. Clutching the cool porcelain edge of the sink, Mollie forced herself to take deep breath.

Zeke was a smart guy. Sure, he'd made the horrible mistake of falling for Lilah in the first place, but Mollie had to believe he'd learned from that disaster. She had to. Because she would no longer be able to keep her silence if Zeke went back to his ex.

"I had a really good time tonight," Josh said as he walked with her toward the front porch.

"So did I," Mollie said, the words true so long as she didn't count the many, many times Zeke had crept into her thoughts or how Lilah Fairchild had ambushed her in ladies' restroom. But neither of those things were Josh's fault.

After her run-in with Lilah, Mollie had lost whatever was left of her appetite, and Josh hadn't pushed her to try more than a single bite of the decadent chocolate lava cake. If he noticed her silence on the ride home, he was gentleman enough not to call her on it.

As they reached the front door, the dogs were already barking their furry heads off. Mollie fought back a groan at the racket her mother had once described as sounding like feeding time for the hyenas at the zoo. "Sorry," she apologized, "I have two new fosters and they're—"

"Excited you're home," Josh filled in. "Who wouldn't be?"

Her dogs, sure, but the thought of anyone else anticipating her return was a foreign concept for Mollie, and she felt her cheeks start to heat. Josh really was a charmer. She fiddled with the zipper of her purse as she sneaked a sideways glance. He was good-looking, too, with that easy smile and those laughing golden eyes. Mollie didn't doubt a dozen or so Spring Forest women would be thrilled at the chance for a goodnight kiss from Josh Sylvester.

If only she felt that spark of excitement sizzle along her nerve endings when she looked his way. If only the sound of his voice shivered across her skin like a cool breeze on a warm day. If only the touch of his hand made her pulse pound and her heart race. If only...

Shoving aside that hopeless train of thought, she turned to face him as they reached the front door. "Thank you again for dinner."

"You're welcome, and I'm only sorry I didn't ask you out sooner."

Maybe it was the benefit of the two glasses of wine, but curiosity had Mollie questioning, "Why didn't you? It wasn't really because my brother warned every guy off ten years ago, was it?"

"Back in high school, maybe, but after that—" He shrugged. "I've never been a guy to poach on another guy's territory."

"Huh?"

"You know. You and Zeke Harper."

"Zeke—" Mollie's face started to flame, and she could only hope the porch's dim lighting disguised the rush of color. "Zeke and I are friends."

"Just friends?" he echoed as he studied her. "Because the two of you have always seemed so…close."

Pity date. Pathetic crush. Even though Lilah had always known how to hit where it hurt, Mollie couldn't deny the painful truth. She wanted more out of life, and she needed to stop hoping that *more* might happen with Zeke.

"We're just friends," she repeated firmly, as much to convince herself as to convince Josh. "I'm the little sister he never wanted."

"If you say so," Josh replied with a fair share of doubt. "But I have sisters, and I don't spend nearly as much time with them as Zeke Harper spends with you."

Chapter Six

Early the next morning, Mollie had barely stumbled out of bed and into the sun-filled kitchen before her cell phone started ringing. Amanda's smiling face flashed across the screen, and for a long, guilt-filled moment, Mollie considered letting the call go to voice mail. Finally, she picked up.

"Well?" So much excitement reverberated through her friend's voice that Mollie was surprised the phone didn't start vibrating in her hand. "How was last night?"

"Last night was…it was good." Tucking the phone into the crook of her shoulder, she focused on dishing out the dogs' morning kibble. Arti and Charlie danced around her feet as if she'd hadn't fed them in weeks while Chief showed a bit more restraint, lying patiently—if a bit pathetically—by his empty bowl. But as she dumped the cup of food inside, he, too, jumped to his feet and wolfed down his breakfast in a matter of seconds.

"Good? That's all you have to say?"

Mollie could have filled her friend in on the flowers Josh had brought, now sitting in the middle of her kitchen table, a bright and beautiful mix of yellow, pink and orange gerbera daisies and rosebuds. Or she could have told Amanda about the restaurant with its romantic ambiance and mouthwatering selections. Or she could have told her friend what she most wanted to hear—that Josh was smart, good-looking, funny... All in all, the perfect date.

So Mollie could only blame a caffeine deficiency for the first words to pop out of her mouth. "Lilah Fairchild's back in town."

After Mollie filled Amanda in on seeing the other woman at the restaurant, her friend said, "Wow, she made such a big deal about leaving Spring Forest after she and Zeke broke up, I never thought she'd come back. You don't think she'll try to rekindle something with Zeke, do you?"

Mollie shrugged even though Amanda couldn't possibly see her. "She said some things along those lines."

"Lilah always did have a way of getting under your skin."

It wasn't her own skin Mollie was worried about. And she didn't care about what the other woman said. But as far as what Lilah had done...

"I can't help worrying about Zeke. He was devastated when they broke up." And then Mollie and Zeke had both been hit with a crushing blow only weeks later when the army delivered the news that Patrick had been killed.

"You know how you're always telling Zeke that you're a grown woman and that you can take care of yourself? Well, that works both ways, hon. Zeke's a big boy. He doesn't need you to protect him."

Mollie's hand tightened on the phone as she thought about just how far she had gone to protect Zeke. "But—"

"No *buts*!" Amanda interrupted. "And when I asked about last night, this isn't exactly what I had in mind." Her earlier excitement had drained away, leaving behind disappointment and a slight tone of hurt.

Sitting on one of the kitchen chairs, Mollie filled her friend in on the parts of the date she figured Amanda actually wanted to hear. When she finished, Amanda practically crowed, "It sounds like the two of you hit it off!"

"Josh made it easy." The date had certainly been more successful than many of her previous attempts. She hadn't spent the entire dinner racking her brain for something to say, feeling so completely uncomfortable in her own skin, wishing she was at home curled up in front of the TV with her dogs.

"He's a good listener and a great storyteller." Summoning up a hint of teasing, Mollie added, "And he had plenty of secrets to spill about when *you* were a kid."

"Oh, please, tell me the two of you had better things to talk about than me!"

At that, Mollie's smile faded a bit. Somehow, she didn't think talking with Josh about *Zeke* would qualify. Slumping against the back of the chair, Mollie swallowed a disheartened sigh. The most memorable part of a date should not be a conversation about her relationship with another man.

And yet she couldn't help wondering. Had Josh picked up on some guy signal she wasn't aware of? Something that said maybe Zeke did see her as more than a little sister?

The thought was almost enough to make Mollie foolishly hold on to hope... Only she'd been holding on to hope—and nothing else—for far too long.

It's about time you got over that pathetic crush...

Unable to keep sitting, Mollie pushed back her chair, sending the dogs who were crowded around the table hoping for some nonexistent scraps, scrambling across the worn linoleum. "We talked about going on a second date and checking out some of the trails around town."

"Oh, that sounds so romantic!"

It does? Mollie certainly hadn't had romance in mind when she made the suggestion. She'd been more focused on coming up with a date where she would actually be able to dress herself and not require her friends' assistance getting ready.

But Amanda sounded so excited...

"I guess it could be romantic," she admitted, thinking of the last time she'd gone hiking. She hadn't noticed one of her shoelaces had come untied and had tripped, landing in an inelegant heap of scraped palms and bloodied knees.

But then again, Zeke had insisted on carrying her back to her car, which was, without a doubt, the most romantic thing to ever happen to her. Closing her eyes, she could still feel the warmth of his soft cotton T-shirt beneath her hands. Still catch a hint of the soap he used combined with the scent of sun-warmed skin. Hear the familiar rumble of his voice as he teased her about her perfect ten dismount.

By the time he drove her back home, she'd been so achingly aware of him, so desperate to believe he felt something of the same desire she felt for him, she actually thought when he crossed the threshold of her house that he would carry her straight to the bedroom where they would finally, *finally* make love.

Instead, he'd headed for the bathroom where he set her down on the edge of the tub to clean her wounds and tape up her palms with cartoon bandages she'd bought for God knew *what* reason. When he was done, he patted her on the knee, just like he had when she'd wiped out on her roller skates in front of his house when she was ten.

Graceful as always, kiddo.

And Mollie had learned then that it was impossible to die of embarrassment, or disappointment…or heartbreak.

"Just think," Amanda was saying, "if things work out between you and Josh, we might end up sisters!"

"Yeah, that would be great," Mollie agreed faintly. She would love to have Amanda for a sister.

Too bad when Josh kissed her good-night, Mollie had felt as though she were kissing her brother.

Zeke raised his hand to knock on Mollie's door, only to hesitate for a moment. He'd hardly slept the night before—uncomfortable with the way he'd left things with Mollie and with the idea of her being out on a date.

He was just looking out for her, the same way he always had, so he didn't understand why she'd be so upset with him. And he did want her to go out, to find someone special to share her life with other than her dogs, so he wasn't sure why *he'd* been so upset with *her*. Shaking off the disquiet, he took a deep breath of the cool morning air and rapped on the door.

Mollie answered only a few seconds later. "Hey, Zeke. What are you doing here?"

Even though her expression was more than a little wary, Zeke exhaled in a huge sigh of relief. Gone was the fancy hair and makeup. Instead, her face was scrubbed clean, her skin highlighted only by a natural glow and the dusting of copper-colored freckles across her cheeks. Her hair was pulled back in a curly pony-tail, and she was wearing a pair of pink pajamas deco-rated with black poodles.

He started to smile at the sight. He didn't think he'd ever seen Mollie in pajamas before. She'd always been an early riser... The bottom fell out of his stomach as he suddenly realized an obvious reason why she may have slept in.

"I, uh—" Zeke swallowed hard. "I'm, um, not inter-rupting anything, am I?"

Mollie shrugged a slender shoulder. "I was just hav-ing breakfast."

In bed? With Josh Sylvester?

Some of his thoughts must have shown on his face, because Mollie's eyes widened. "Oh, my—" Reaching out, she socked him in the shoulder just like she'd done when she was a kid. "It was a *first* date, Zeke!"

"I know but—" She'd looked so gorgeous the night before. What man wouldn't have wanted to take her to bed?

"But what?" she demanded as she stalked away, leaving him with little choice but to follow her into the cozy comfort of her living room.

The small space was decorated with an eclectic and colorful mix of secondhand furniture Mollie had dis-covered at consignment shops and thrift stores through-out North Carolina. He'd taken more than a few trips across the state with her to haul her trash-to-treasure finds back to her house.

Of course, if she and Josh hit it off, Mollie wouldn't need him for that anymore.

"Oh, that's right!" She stopped in the middle of the room and turned to face him. She threw her hands up into the air before planting her fists on her slender hips. "You know me so well! You must have realized I was out for some kind of wild affair!"

Wild affair.

The words kept bouncing off his stunned brain in more and more dangerous combinations. *Mollie...affair. Mollie...wild.*

Truth was, she looked a little wild right then. With her red hair ablaze from the morning sunlight streaming through the lace-curtained windows. With aquamarine sparks flying from her eyes. With her chest heaving beneath the black cotton tank top.

But he didn't think of Mollie that way. He couldn't. Zeke still remembered how Patrick had warned off all the guys in Spring Forest before he left for basic training, telling them to stay away from his little sister. Zeke had laughed about it at the time. After all, Mollie had been a kid.

Zeke wasn't laughing now. And Mollie was all grown-up.

Her pajamas might not have been the sexy silk negligees he'd seen in the storefront window, yet that hardly mattered. Her thin cotton tank top outlined the feminine shape of her breasts. The drawstring bottoms she wore had slipped down on one side to reveal the hollow curve of her hip. And even without the added benefit of makeup, her lips were a rosy pink that Zeke was suddenly dying to feel against his.

Mollie McFadden was all woman. He wasn't sure

how he'd turned a blind eye for all of these years, but now he couldn't bring himself to look away.

"Is that why you came over this morning? To see if my dinner date lasted until breakfast?" she demanded.

"No, I—" he started, with no idea where he was going. It was a feeling he hated. Zeke always wanted to have a plan in place and a backup plan, just in case.

Mollie crossed her arms, waiting for him to say something—anything—but the move only lowered the lace-trimmed edge of her tank ever so slightly to reveal even more of the delicate swell of creamy flesh, and Zeke's tongue stuck to the roof of his mouth.

He dragged his attention away and struggled to suck in a deep breath, only to have the air knocked right out of him as his gaze locked onto one of the pictures on Mollie's mantel.

Patrick, in full dress uniform, stared back at him from inside a silver frame.

In most of the pictures, Patrick was smiling out from behind the glass, a hint of laughter in his blue eyes. That was the Patrick Zeke tried to remember. The friend he'd had from the day the two of them met in the second grade.

But in the graduation photo, Patrick was not smiling. His serious expression revealed the hard work and sacrifice that had been required to don that uniform. That was Patrick McFadden, sergeant first class, the soldier who had given his life defending his country and who had given Zeke one task.

Look out for my kid sister.

Zeke couldn't do that if he let himself get too close. Friendship was one thing, but to cross a line into something more than that—he couldn't let that happen.

Seeing Patrick's photo was a stark reminder for Zeke

to focus on the reason he'd stopped by Mollie's house. And it had nothing to do with finding out how her date had gone with Josh Sylvester. Nothing at all.

"Look, I didn't come here to talk about your date. I was talking with Matt Fielding the other day about Bobby Doyle." At Mollie's questioning glance, he added, "He owns the auto-body shop where Matt's working."

"Oh, I think Claire might have mentioned him. He's a former soldier, too, isn't he?"

"He is. Along with their love of cars, Matt and Bobby also have their years of service in common." After filling Mollie in on their conversation, he said, "Bobby isn't ready to admit he needs help, but I've seen how service dogs have helped some of the other vets at the center."

"That's a great idea, Zeke," Mollie said, compassion softening her features. "But service dogs require specialized training and—"

"The waitlists are long," he filled in. "So I've learned. But I've also seen how much Sparkle and Hank have helped Matt, and neither of those dogs have had any training beyond basic obedience. I'm hoping that if you could help me find the right dog for Bobby, that it would—well, at least give him a four-legged friend to talk to since he isn't ready to talk to anyone else."

Let it go, Zeke... I'll talk when I'm ready.

Zeke had let it go. He'd let Patrick go back to his unit, back on patrol. He'd let his friend go straight to his death.

Guilt and loss and regret festered in the dark void his friend had left behind, and Zeke wouldn't—couldn't—give up until he did everything he could to help Bobby. It was too late for Patrick but not for Bobby and the other soldiers in the support group. His fingers clenched, but instead of closing into an empty fist, they dug into warm, soft fur. Startled, he glanced down. He hadn't even noticed that Charlie, the yellow Lab, had settled by his side, her tail swishing across the hardwood floors.

"I think I just may know the perfect dog," Mollie said softly.

Zeke looked up in surprise even as he continued to pet the dog leaning so patiently, so steadfastly against his leg. "Charlie? But what about Chief? I thought the two of them belonged together."

Even though Mollie's lips lifted, Zeke didn't know if he'd ever seen a smile so sad. "Sometimes you just have to move on to someone new."

Move on... Zeke wasn't sure why the finality of that had his heart starting to pound. She was still talking about the dogs, wasn't she?

Even if she were, Zeke knew last night had the power to change things at a time when he wanted everything to stay the same. His friendship with Mollie was a last, fragile connection to Patrick. As tough as it had been losing Patrick, Zeke couldn't imagine what it would be like to lose Mollie, too.

"Mollie, about last night…" He took a step closer. "Seeing you…well, it took me by surprise."

Her arms lowered, and she ran her tongue over her lower lip. "It did?"

Her gaze softened as she stared up at him. Had he taken another step closer or had she? Zeke wasn't sure but suddenly they stood toe-to-toe. All the freckles she'd tried to hide the night before were scattered like pixie dust over her cheeks, and he had the crazy thought that if he brushed a thumb over her skin he might somehow capture some of that magic for himself...

"It made me realize—"

"Realize what, Zeke?" she whispered.

"That Josh Sylvester is—"

Wrong for you. Completely, utterly, unfailingly wrong for you.

Only he couldn't say that. He had no right to say that. Not when friendship was all he could offer. Not when Mollie deserved so much more.

"...a lucky guy."

Mollie's jaw dropped and then snapped shut as she took the sudden step back that Zeke hadn't been able to take himself.

"I just want you to be happy, Mollie."

"Right. Happy."

Was it his imagination or did she sound anything but happy?

Mollie turned away for a moment to pet Charlie, who at some point had abandoned him to take Mollie's side over his. Straightening, she met his gaze with a bright smile. "Now all we need to do is plan that double date!"

Chapter Seven

Mollie wasn't sure how she made it out of the living room. Mumbling an excuse about needing to get dressed, she'd practically sprinted down the hall to the solitude of her bedroom. The comfort of her ruffled canopy bed beckoned, and she wanted nothing more than to throw herself onto the white chenille bedspread and give in to the tears burning at the back of her throat.

Josh is a lucky guy.

And she was the world's biggest idiot.

Mollie yanked at a drawer so hard she was surprised she didn't pull the thing right out of the dresser. Honestly, how many times was she going to fool herself into thinking Zeke felt something more than friendship for her before she finally got a clue?

Wasn't...going...to...happen.

And she needed to get over it. To move on. Her eyes burned as she stripped off her pajamas and tossed them into the hamper. She purposely grabbed her oldest and grubbiest Best Friends T-shirt and ragged denim jeans. No need to dress up since Lucky Josh wasn't around to see her.

She tightened her lopsided ponytail and slipped her feet into her favorite pair of tennis shoes before heading back out to find Zeke. She didn't have her dogs' uncanny aptitude for sensing someone new in their space. Instead, she followed the sound of laughter and play growls to find Zeke on the floor with all three dogs crowded around him.

He flashed her a crooked grin as he glanced up at her and had to duck to avoid taking a tail right in his face. Though she longed to hold on to her anger as a shield, she'd never been able to stay mad at Zeke. He climbed to his feet, but not before giving each dog a final pat. The hounds, including Chief, crowded around him, still eager for attention.

Mollie knew exactly how they felt.

Gesturing to the rescue dog, Zeke said, "I can't believe how far he's come already."

"Unfortunately, a lot of dogs don't do well in a shelter environment. Dogs like a quieter home with set routines and time to spend with their own people."

"You've done an amazing job with him."

Mollie shook her head. "Really I had little to do with it. It was all Chief and Charlie." And it would be hard to separate the two, but she'd meant what she said earlier.

Sometimes life gave you little choice but to move on.

"Do you really think Charlie would be able to help Bobby?"

"Like you said, Charlie would be a great companion dog, just as she is. As far as acting as a service dog, I think with the right training, she'd be perfect." The bigger question was, would *she* be able to provide that training? Dozens of dogs had graduated from her programs, but obedience and agility weren't the same as training a service dog. Still, a thrum of anticipation had nerves in her belly fluttering.

Had Patrick still been alive, he would have encouraged her to take this chance. He would have seen the challenge as not only an opportunity to give back but also a way for her to push herself. He'd always been her biggest supporter, and Mollie was ready to prove— if only to herself—that he'd been right to put his faith in her.

"I'd really like to work with her to see if there's even more she could do to help Bobby with his PTSD."

"You'd do that?" Zeke's eyes lit, and he took a step forward.

One Mollie countered by stepping back. Not again. She wasn't going to make a fool of herself again. Just because for a split second it looked like Zeke wanted to reach out, sweep her into his arms and kiss her, she knew better.

Some of the excitement in his expression dimmed as he ended up running the hand he'd lifted through his short hair. "That's—that's great, Mollie. How soon do you think you can get started?"

"Well, I'll have to read up on the type of training Charlie will need. How to teach her to recognize Bobby's cues and what responses he'll need from her."

"I hope this isn't going to be too much for you to take on. I didn't even think about that when I asked. I was just thinking of Bobby and wanting to find some way to help him."

A shadow crossed his face. Helping people was so much more than a job to Zeke. Was it any wonder she couldn't stay angry with him? Mollie swallowed a sigh. Was it any wonder she couldn't stop loving him?

Shoving the depressing thought aside, Mollie straightened her shoulders. This wasn't about her or about Zeke. This was about helping Bobby Doyle, a soldier like her brother who had sacrificed to serve his country.

"Don't worry about me, Zeke. I can handle this." Thinking about her brother, she added, "In fact, I've already been doing some new training with Arti lately."

"With Arti?"

Mollie didn't miss the slightly skeptical lift to his brow.

Hearing her name, the long-eared dog gave a quick bark. After butting her head against Zeke's legs a few times, she rolled onto her back at his feet, shamelessly begging for a belly rub when he didn't respond to her first oh, so subtle hints.

With a soft snort, Zeke gave in and bent down to run his hands over the goofy dog's rib cage and belly. Loving it, Arti snorted and groaned, twisting from side to side as she rubbed her back on the area rug, blissfully soaking up the attention.

"Hey, she's smarter than she looks," Mollie argued. She couldn't blame Zeke for questioning Arti's abilities. Her furry friend had a well-earned reputation as a crazy hound dog—obnoxious bark, stubborn streak, food obsession and all. But she also had genetics on her side and a nose that wouldn't quit. "After all, she's got *you* right where she wants you."

Despite the brave words, nerves danced in her belly. Scent work wasn't the same as service work, but all training was based on rewarding the dog for the wanted behavior. She and Arti had worked hard, and she really wanted to impress Zeke.

She'd hoped, when Zeke unexpectedly showed up at her door last night, that he would be impressed then, too. She'd ended up disappointed, but putting on a dress and makeup and a pair of heels, that wasn't really her. This, training dogs, this was who she really was.

"Give me half an hour," Mollie vowed as Zeke pushed to his feet, "and I'll show you what this girl can do."

Glancing at his watch as he stood with Arti on the back porch, Zeke wasn't sure what to expect when the ten minutes were up. Mollie had left him with instructions to give Arti the command to "go find" before handing him a familiar dark blue Best Friends T-shirt emblazoned with her company logo—an outline of a cartoon dog sailing through a hoop. The flapping ears and streaming tail of the dog in the image made it more than clear that Arti was the inspiration. He was a little surprised Mollie hadn't added some kind of cape—like the one worn by the old Wonder Dog cartoon.

The *wonder dog* in question was currently making a guttural groan as she scratched at one of those long ears with a back paw.

Zeke shook his head a little as he waited for the timer on his smart watch to go off.

"You really think you can find our girl using this, huh?" he asked the dog as he waved the shirt in his hand.

Years ago, Mollie had given him one exactly like it, but as he rubbed the cotton between his fingers, he didn't remember the shirt he owned being quite so soft. And it was kind of crazy, knowing that Mollie had pulled the garment from the hamper and not straight from her body, but he swore the material felt heated, as if clinging to the warmth of her skin.

She'd told him that she didn't want to use an article of clothing that had been recently washed as the scent wouldn't be as strong. Her cheeks had turned a little red as she'd handed him the shirt, as though she was embarrassed to be literally airing her dirty laundry in front of him. Which was nuts considering how long they'd been friends.

Whatever she did, Mollie gave it her all. She worked hard—training her dogs, volunteering at the rescue, re-modeling her house. As she'd told him the other day, she wasn't afraid to get dirty. But the only scent he caught from the soft material was fresh linen fabric softener and a hint of wildflowers that smelled like Mollie and Mollie alone...

The alarm on his wrist sounded and Zeke jumped, flinching as if he'd been caught—well, doing exactly what he'd been doing. Sniffing Mollie's clothes.

What the hell was wrong with him?

Arti made a low sound in her throat, as close as he'd heard the dog ever come to a growl, and Zeke's face heated even more. "Yeah, I know, I know. *You're* sup-posed to be the crazy hound dog."

Shutting off the timer, he bent down to the dog's side, placed the shirt in front of her nose and gave the command. "Go find, Ar—"

He barely got the words out before Arti lunged off the porch, nearly dislocating his shoulder as he stumbled down the steps after her. Once they hit the ground, she slowed slightly, sweeping her nose along the ground, her ears practically dragging through the long grass.

Zeke wanted to give the dog a hint by leading her to the back gate, knowing that Mollie had left the yard, but he held back. This was Arti's—and Mollie's—chance to show what the dog could do, and he wasn't going to rob either one of that.

He just hoped Arti was as good at this as her owner thought she was.

Though the area around Spring Forest had spread out into planned communities, including the highly popular Kingdom Creek, as young professionals with families moved out of the nearby cities for a slower paced, more rural lifestyle, the area north of town still held fast to its surrounding forests and creeks.

The open spaces and lack of close neighbors were the main reasons Mollie had bought the run-down house. Though both he and Patrick had encouraged her to start the business, Patrick had worried about Mollie living so far from town and all on her own.

"I'll be fine," Mollie had insisted. "I've got Arti with me, and she'd never let anything happen to me."

Only now, Arti wasn't with Mollie. The dog was with Zeke, and as five minutes stepping over rocks, ducking under low-hanging branches, pushing through dense bushes turned to ten and then to fifteen, Zeke's pulse started to pound. He was in good enough shape that the distance and the terrain shouldn't have been enough to elevate his heart rate.

Wiping his free hand across his sweating fore-head, he doggedly followed Arti's wagging tail. He should have insisted Mollie take a phone with her. Even though cell service could sometimes be spotty in this area, it would have been better than nothing. As Arti started to circle back, nose to the ground, sniffing every rock, every leaf, every bush, Zeke felt his patience begin to wane.

What if Mollie really had gotten lost? Was he honestly supposed to trust her rescue to a dog who was terrified of the vacuum cleaner and more than once had nearly knocked herself silly whacking her head into a piece of furniture while chasing her own tail? Could Arti really do this?

I can do this, Zeke.

Mollie's stubborn voice echoed through his mind.

How many times had she said those words over the years? As recently as a few days ago, when he'd questioned her about bringing Chief and Charlie home with her…to as far back as the day they'd rescued Shadow.

Mollie still swore he'd saved the dog's life by jumping into the rushing stream. But when Zeke jumped into the water, his only thought had been to save *Mollie.*

He'd always been a strong swimmer, but the normally gentle stream had been swollen from record-breaking spring rains. The fast-moving rapids had threatened to overwhelm him as he fought to pull Mollie and the dog to safety.

His muscles had burned with the effort, and Mollie had tried to help, her skinny legs kicking furiously, choking as the undertow dragged her down, still clinging to the struggling puppy.

Let it go, Mollie! You've got to let the dog go!

With her red hair streaming across her face and her freckles stark against her pale skin, she'd shouted back at him. *I can do this, Zeke!*

And she had. She'd held on to the puppy, he'd held on to her, and somehow the three of them had collapsed together on the muddy bank. Waterlogged, gasping for breath and totally exhausted.

Too tired to move, the poor puppy had still managed to lick both of their faces, tail wagging in gratitude. Mollie had laughed, pushing her sopping curls out of her face as she gazed over the puppy's head at him. "You did it, Zeke." Her eyes had glowed as she added, "You saved her."

As a somewhat geeky sixteen-year-old, he'd basked in her admiration, thoroughly enjoying her preteen case of hero worship. He'd liked the idea of being there when she needed him. He still liked the idea...even if Mollie didn't need him quite so much anymore.

As for thinking of him as a hero, that light in Mollie's eyes when she looked at him would forever fade if she knew the truth about Patrick's last visit home and how completely Zeke had failed her brother.

Let it go, Zeke...

He stumbled as he caught his foot on a rock on the uneven ground.

He didn't have the strength, the tenacity, the *courage* Mollie had had as a twelve-year-old girl.

Zeke was jarred back to the present as Arti let out a sudden unmistakable howl. The dog charged forward, crashing through the underbrush and practically dragging Zeke along behind him. He had to fight the urge to try to bring the dog to heel, instead following Arti's lead and doing his best just to keep up.

Hoping to hell the dog hadn't caught wind of a squirrel, he muttered, "Go find, girl. Go find."

The dog dove into a thick cluster of underbrush, still baying at the top of her canine lungs, but even with all that racket, Zeke heard a sound that set his blood singing in his veins.

Ducking down, he caught sight of Mollie huddled between a cluster of bright green winterberry bushes, her head tipped back in laughter as she tried to avoid her dog's exuberant and drooly greeting. Mollie had clearly meant it when she said she was going to hide. As she climbed out from between the bushes, she had a few leaves caught in her curls, a smudge of dirt on one cheek and mud stains on the knees of her jeans.

He'd never seen her look happier...or more beautiful.

"Good job! Who's the best hound dog? Who's my best girl ever?"

Catching sight of Zeke on the back end of the leash, Mollie grinned up at him and all he could think was... *My best girl ever.*

"I told you she could do it," she bragged as she pushed to her feet. She took the hand he offered to help her up, only to stumble slightly when he accidentally pulled too hard...on purpose.

She landed against his chest with a slight exhale of breath, her blue-green eyes wide as she gazed up at him, her hands clutching at his shoulders and her lips parted in surprise.

"I never should have doubted it, Mollie."

He never should have doubted her.

They'd known each other for years, and yet he couldn't help feeling he was seeing her for the first time. How strong and beautiful she was, inside and out.

"Zeke..." Her delicate throat moved as she swallowed, her voice trembling on his name, and even though he and Arti were the ones who'd found Mollie, he didn't know when he had felt more lost. He was drowning. So he did the only thing that made sense. He grabbed Mollie and held on.

But the minute his mouth closed over hers, a tidal wave of desire crashed over him. He was swirling through eddies of emotion, tossed in one direction and then another...until Mollie reached up and wrapped her arms around his shoulders.

Her lips parted beneath his, and it no longer mattered if he couldn't breathe. Who needed air when he had this? When he had the taste, the sweetness, the warmth of her surrounding him. Grounding him at a time when he didn't know which way to turn. Centering all he was, all he had to give, in this one amazing kiss.

She ran her fingers through his hair as his hands discovered the supple curve of her spine and the softness of her hips. He pulled her body tighter to his, that softness a seductive contrast as his body hardened to the point of pain.

In the back of his mind, his conscience protested. *This is Mollie... Kissing her is wrong!* But his body, thrumming with desire, disagreed. This was Mollie. And nothing could be more right...

The unexpected kiss, after so many years of waiting, hoping, dreaming, caught Mollie so off guard that at first she couldn't move, couldn't think. Her body felt as stiff and still as those mannequins in the store windows. But then, like some wish had been granted, she came to glorious, magical life in Zeke's hands as he finally, finally realized she was a real girl.

She lifted her arms to wrap them around his neck. His shoulders were as strong and solid as she'd always imagined, and she'd been imagining for so long... Wondering if he would taste like the rich, dark coffee he favored…if the thick hair that brushed against his collar was as soft as it looked…if he would kiss her in the same fierce, possessive way he had protected her for all these years…

She discovered all of that and more.

Most of all, she discovered that wanting Zeke Harper from afar was nothing compared to wanting him with his fingers digging into her flesh, his tongue staking claim to her mouth, his hardened body pressing into hers.

Mine, mine, mine! The words matched the rapid, vital beat of her heart, but she knew it wasn't true. Her heart had always been something of a liar where Zeke Harper was concerned.

He broke the kiss to suck in a sudden breath, but Mollie didn't need air. She could live on the lightheaded, intoxicating way he made her feel. Too greedy to lose the contact of her mouth against his flesh, his taste on her tongue, she kissed her way along his jaw to the strong column of his neck. His pulse leaped as she parted her lips, his heart pounding in a rhythm so close to her own, she could almost believe the wild, reckless beats had become one.

"Mollie!" He groaned out her name once and then again. But the second time sounded different. Like a sleepwalker waking from a dream, uncertain where they were, what they were doing, who they were with…

For a long moment, he stood still, his breath still rasping in her ear, his chest still heaving against her breasts, their limbs still so closely entwined. But then he pulled away—a few inches maybe, less than a foot, but it may as well have been a mile.

"I'm sorry, Mollie," Zeke said, his voice deeper than usual and with a ragged edge she'd never heard before.

He closed his eyes for a moment before whispering, "I didn't mean—"

At his words, all the life drained out of Mollie. Her arms to drop to her sides. Wooden…and empty.

He didn't mean it.

"It was—a mistake."

Just when she thought she couldn't possibly feel any worse, Mollie thought dismally, swallowing against the ache of tears grabbing hold of her throat. *A mistake.* Zeke had called the most wonderful kiss she'd ever shared a mistake. A mistake he hadn't even meant to make. At least, not with her, the kid sister he'd never wanted.

She stared at him silently until he ran a hand through his hair, and then she had to look away. She could still feel the chestnut strands sifting through her fingers. Running her tongue over her lower lip, Mollie tried to recapture his taste. Only when she realized what she was doing did she snap out of the sensual daze.

Her cheeks, flushed only a moment ago with passion, now burned with embarrassed humiliation. Kneeling down, Mollie grabbed Arti's leash and started back down the trail at a near run, as if super speed could turn back time and wipe away the kiss. Zeke jogged along beside her, his longer stride easily keeping pace.

"Mollie—"

"Don't. Whatever you're going to say, don't." Whatever apology, whatever regret, whatever bright idea about fixing her up with some other guy Zeke had, he could keep it to himself.

Chapter Eight

"Hey, Mom." Zeke followed the scent of yeasty rolls and cinnamon into the kitchen. Though his parents had recently remodeled the space, the mouthwatering smell of his mother's cooking always took him back to his childhood.

Spotting a pan of sugar-glazed buns cooling on the large granite island, he headed in that direction. Unfortunately, his mother knew his sweet tooth all too well. As trim as ever in denim capris and a blue-striped T-shirt, her short brown hair only starting to turn gray, Margaret Harper still had all the instincts of a school teacher. Without even turning around from where she stood at the glass-top stove, she swatted him with a dishtowel as he reached out.

"Those are for our guests, so hands off!" she said, referring to the two dozen or so friends invited to a barbecue that afternoon.

"I think I should try one out first, you know, just to make sure they're okay."

"Because when have my cinnamon rolls not been more than okay?" she challenged with a glance over her shoulder. For Margaret, the process of baking was a fascinating mix of math and science, and Zeke was more than willing to reap the benefits of her delicious experiments. "Besides, you don't want to ruin your appetite."

"Not possible."

"Something smells wonderful!" John Harper complimented his wife as he stepped into the kitchen. An older version of Zeke with the same lean build, brown hair and hazel eyes, his father looked very much like the history professor he was—tall and distinguished— even when casually dressed in khaki pants and a red polo shirt.

"Cinnamon buns *for our guests*." Margaret stressed the words when—like father, like son—John headed toward the dessert. "And I also have some baked beans warming on the stove. Now, if we just had something more to go with them."

John grumbled good-naturedly beneath his breath as he opened the refrigerator door and start pulling out the packages of hot dogs and burgers. More familiar with his parents' kitchen than with his own, Zeke stepped into the walk-in pantry and grabbed the superstore-sized packages of paper plates, napkins and red plastic cups off the shelves.

"How was your week?" his mother called from her spot at the stove.

"It was…good."

Margaret glanced over her shoulder as he backed out of the pantry and set the supplies on the kitchen table. "Well, that sounds about as convincing as the night I decided to try my hand at Thai food."

His father shook his head as he grabbed the ketchup and mustard from the fridge door. "I swear I had heartburn for weeks."

Heartburn… That wasn't exactly the way Zeke would describe how he was feeling, but then again, it wasn't that far off. Not that he was about talk to his parents about the kiss he and Mollie had shared.

A mistake, he told himself for the hundredth time as he grabbed a soda from the open fridge and popped the top. The most inappropriate, unacceptable, unforgettable, irresistible mistake he'd made in his life.

Buying himself some time, he took a long drink from the cold can. The carbonated fizz did little to wash away the sour taste of guilt lingering in the back of his throat. "It was fine, really."

When it became clear he wasn't going to elaborate, his mother gave the beans a final stir and replaced the lid. "I went to get my hair done on Monday."

Assuming that was some kind of hint, his father nodded. "Looks real nice," he said, waving a pair of tongs as he headed out to fire up the grill.

Margaret rolled her eyes even as she called after him, "Thank you, dear."

Zeke, however, had the feeling his mother was going somewhere else with that segue. The door had barely closed behind his father before she said, "While I was there, I ran into Joann Anderson and she said she and Herb tried that new seafood restaurant… You know, the one over in Raleigh?"

Zeke nodded. He and Mollie had talked about going there. It was something of a tradition between the two of them—to wait and experience a trendy restaurant or blockbuster movie or buzz-worthy museum exhibit together. A few months ago, they'd gone to a pizza joint that had just opened up in Hendrix. The old-fashioned parlor had an arcade filled with retro games—everything from back-in-the-day video games to air hockey and Skee-Ball.

Bells and whistles and the sound of explosions had reverberated throughout the place, and the two of them had raced from game to game, laughing and trying to beat each other like they were still a couple of kids.

But now, as he thought of taking Mollie out, reclaiming some nostalgic piece of childhood didn't come to mind. Instead, his thoughts went to candlelit tables, soft music and an air of romance as he imagined sitting across a linen-draped table with Mollie looking like she did when—

"Mollie was there with that handsome Josh Sylvester."

Zeke coughed as he half swallowed, half choked on the soda. "Mollie and—"

"And Josh," his mother repeated as if Zeke hadn't heard her well enough the first time. "I think he was in your class in high school, wasn't he?"

He had been. Along with being *that handsome*, Josh Sylvester had also been smart and popular, homecoming king and star of the basketball team. Meanwhile, Zeke had been the typical nerd, the overachieving geek hiding behind thick glasses and thicker stacks of books.

Sure, the hard work and brains had paid off as he'd gone on to college and a career he loved, and LASIK surgery in his early twenties had taken care of the glasses, but still...

He found himself asking, "So, is Mollie coming today?"

His mother shot him a puzzled look. "As far as I know. Wouldn't she have said something to you yesterday if she wasn't?"

"The subject didn't come up." Probably because they'd been too busy with…other things.

"Hmm, well, I suppose she could have plans. Maybe seeing Josh again. Of course, there's no reason why Mollie couldn't bring him along today."

"Yeah, that'd be great," Zeke said, rubbing at the sudden ache in his chest.

Just about as great as his mother's attempt at Thai food.

Remembering that he, too, had invited other guests, Zeke said, "I did ask Matt Fielding and Claire Asher." He had also extended an invitation to Bobby Doyle and his family, but the former army sergeant had refused, saying he had other plans.

Zeke hoped that truly was the case.

"Oh, good. I ran into the two of them at The Granary the other day," his mother said, referring to the grain factory that had been converted to a popular shopping area. "They looked so happy together." Margaret paused for a moment, the wooden spoon in her hand slowing to a stop as she gazed out the window to the Fairchild house next door. "It's so romantic, isn't it, the way they've reunited after so many years apart…?"

His mother fell silent for a moment, and Zeke's stomach started to churn.

"Claire and Matt are so fortunate to have this second chance."

"Yep." He agreed entirely when it came to his friend's romance. But Zeke had no interest in rekindling any kind of flame with Lilah Fairchild now that he'd heard she was back in town.

Not after getting burned big-time.

Still, he hated seeing the far-off look in his mother's eyes. Two years ago, the Fairchilds wouldn't have missed a Harper barbecue. But Lilah's parents and his parents had hardly talked since the breakup, a decade of friendship ruined.

He didn't blame Lilah's parents for taking her side, but he wasn't sure how he'd ended up the bad guy. During those last few weeks in March, less than three months from their planned wedding date, he'd sensed something was off. Lilah had seemed distant, uncommunicative, until she finally told him she needed some space… Which turned out to be around four thousand miles of ocean as the next thing he knew, she'd moved to France and returned his engagement ring in the mail.

For the longest time, he had tried to figure out what had gone wrong. What *he'd* done wrong. Had he tried too hard? Not hard enough? What signs had he missed that could have prevented him from making such a big mistake in the first place? For all his questions, he found few answers, so he took from the experience the only thing he could.

Ever since Lilah, he'd kept his dating life separate from his friends and family. It was much simpler that way, and when it came to women, Zeke didn't want any added complications.

Like the complication of crossing the line and kissing his best friend.

With a glance at the clock on the microwave, his mother sighed. "Can you see what is taking your father so long? If he doesn't have that grill going soon, we'll be feeding our guests uncooked hot dogs."

Jerking his mind from the memory of Mollie in his arms, he said, "Technically, hot dogs are already cooked." Catching his mother's look, he quickly added, "But I'll go check."

As he stepped out into his parents' backyard, memories of the hours he'd spent there with Patrick assailed him, as bright and blinding as the sun overhead. Splashing and laughter in the cool, clear water of the pool. The bounce and thud of the basketball against the backboard, peppered with seriously foul trash-talking during their ultra-competitive pick-up games. Hanging out in the shade of the redwood pergola, eating their way through endless bags of greasy burgers and fries as they talked about sport and girls and what they were going to do with the rest of their lives…

Look out for my little sis, would ya, Z?

And Zeke knew there was no way around the truth.

He hadn't just crossed a line of friendship when he'd pulled Mollie into his arms.

He'd overshot the boundaries by a country mile.

Mollie had her doubts about going to the Harpers' barbecue. Several times during the drive over, she'd been tempted to turn the SUV around, go home and eat the entire pan of double-dark-chocolate brownies herself. In one sitting. With a vanilla ice cream chaser.

She didn't know how she was supposed to act, seeing Zeke for the first time since their kiss in the woods. As much as she'd like to play everything cool, as if she went around kissing guys all the time, Mollie doubted she had what it took to pull off such a blasé attitude.

She'd dreamed for years of kissing Zeke, from her preteen days when she barely knew what kissing was about, right up to the moment a few days ago when, as a grown woman, she'd *thought* she knew what it was about. But kissing Zeke was better than any dream, bet-

ter than any reality of the kisses she'd had in the past...
until she'd seen the look of near horror on Zeke's face
and the whole thing turned into a nightmare.

But she still managed a smile as she stepped into
his parents' kitchen and his mother greeted her with a
hug. "Mollie!" As she accepted the plate of brownies,
Margaret scolded, "You didn't have to bring anything."

Mollie had always liked Margaret Harper. Though
she had a no-nonsense reputation with her high school
math students, at home she was warm and welcoming.
Far more so than Mollie's own mother. "I don't mind.
I like baking and—"

"Zeke likes eating."

Her heart cramped a little as Zeke's mother finished
the age-old line Mollie always gave for why she liked
to cook so much. "That's right."

"And don't you look lovely! Is that dress new?"

Brushing her suddenly sweating palms over the flow-
ered skirt, as if she could somehow turn the dress into
her typical jeans and T-shirt, Mollie's face heated. "Um,
yeah, it is."

Oh, God, was it totally obvious that she was trying
too hard when—where it came to Zeke—she wasn't
supposed to be trying at all?

"You know, Zeke seemed worried that you weren't
coming today. I couldn't think of a reason why you
wouldn't..." Margaret's smile turned a little teasing
as she set the brownies aside. "Although I thought you
might bring Josh Sylvester with you."

"You—you did?" Mollie asked, surprised Zeke had
told his mother about her date.

"Sure. The more the merrier, right?"

"Right," Mollie said hollowly. After all, Zeke had
already suggested a double date. Why would he have

a problem with her bringing Josh to a Harper friends and family barbecue? And it wasn't like he'd kissed her, completely ruining her for Josh or any man, just the day before!

His mother frowned as she caught sight of Mollie's expression. "Is everything all right?"

Trying to keep the steam from blowing out her ears, Mollie forced a smile. "Just fine."

Margaret lifted a brow in question. "Funny, if I didn't know better, I'd think you and Zeke both were suffering from a serious case of Thai food."

Standing with his father at the smoking, sizzling grill, Zeke didn't realize how closely he'd been watching the back door until Mollie stepped outside. His heart did a slow roll in his chest as he caught sight of her. She looked lovely—as fresh and sunny as the summer day in a white, halter-style dress. The bodice hugged the curves of her breasts while leaving her arms bare, and the pink-and-purple flowers embroidered along the skirt instantly drew his eyes to her toned calves.

His hand clenched around the metal tongs he held as he waited… The wave of relief rushing through him when he saw she was alone left him weak-kneed. Bad enough to hear from Mollie—and oh, yeah, *his mom*— about her date with Josh Sylvester. The last thing he wanted was to see the two of them together.

Except…hadn't he been the one to encourage Mollie to go out more? Like she'd told him the night of her date, the idea had been his to begin with. So why did the whole thing bother him so much?

Shoving the thought aside, he turned to his father. "You okay here?"

His dad nodded. "Your mother can rest assured that we will not be serving uncooked hot dogs."

Wincing at the flash of heat from a sudden flare-up, Zeke hung the tongs on the side of the grill. "Yeah." He eyed the charred and blistered dogs. "I think we're safe there."

Wondering if it was too late to order pizza for the crowd gathered in the backyard, Zeke left the shaded outdoor kitchen and jogged across the lush lawn. He greeted some of their friends and neighbors along the way as they called out his name, stopping only long enough to shake a hand or to let them know about the drinks and snacks lining the tables set up in the shade of the giant oaks. The instant Mollie spotted him, her own steps slowed and the wariness in her blue-green eyes hit him straight in the chest.

She'd never, not in the almost twenty years that he'd known her, looked anything but happy to see him. "Mollie…" he began, only to find himself at a complete loss as to where to go from there.

She tilted her head, nodding in the direction of the inferno of a grill. "Your dad need a fire extinguisher yet?"

"It's getting close. I have both the fire department and the pizza place on speed dial, just in case."

She nodded in response, but the pressure in his chest failed to ease. The familiar jokes were hitting all the right notes, but like an out of tune piano, none of the words rang true. As she turned to walk away, Zeke caught her arm. "Mollie, I want—"

His words cut off as she turned back to him, her eyes huge in her lovely face, her skin soft and warm beneath his touch. She'd left her hair down, the reddish curls tumbling against her freckled shoulders, and his fingers itched to sift through the silken strands.

You, his subconscious urged. *I want you.*

As he floundered for something to say, her chin lifted. Aware of the people gathered in laughing, chatting groups nearby, she leaned close enough for him to see the anger striking sparks in her eyes. "If you apologize for kissing me again, I will put some of those self-defense moves you and Patrick taught me back in junior high to good use, and then, Zeke Harper, you really will have something to be sorry about!"

Zeke couldn't help but smile at what was such a Mollie response. Smiling was probably not his best move, though, considering the way her gaze narrowed even more and how she seemed to be eyeing up his package for a quick delivery from her knee. "No apologies," he promised as he held his ground, resisting the urge to take a sudden backward step out of range. "But I want to explain."

Mollie crossed her arms. "Turn that big brain of yours off for a minute, would you? I don't need a kiss explained to me. I'm well aware of what happens between two consenting adults."

Zeke might have been all about consenting, but he wasn't feeling very adult at the moment. Not when he wanted to clap his hands over his ears to keep from hearing what else Mollie might have to say about her own experience on the subject. He was still having a difficult time, as it was, thinking of Mollie *that* way. Sex was the last thing they should be talking about—thinking about—in front of friends and family!

"I want to explain," he practically shouted, loud enough that a few of those friends and family members glanced his way. Looking around at the people gathered in his parents' backyard, he couldn't help thinking of the couple conspicuously absent. "Two years ago, the Fairchilds wouldn't have dreamed of missing this barbecue."

For ten years, his parents and Lilah's did everything together. Their dads had been golf buddies; their mothers co-chairs of just about every charity and event in the small town. "But all that changed after my broken engagement."

Not only were the Fairchilds no longer friends with his parents, but they could almost be considered enemies. Instead of working together on the various boards, now Mrs. Fairchild ran against his mother at every opportunity. Lilah's father, a powerful lawyer in Raleigh, had actually threatened to sue for monetary and emotional damages thanks to all the money the Fairchilds had doled out in advance payments on an over-the-top expensive wedding that had never taken place.

In the end, Zeke had forked over half the costs for the nonrefundable deposits. All in all, a small price to pay. He'd been such a fool, and one of his main beliefs in life was that anyone who didn't learn from their mistakes was bound to repeat them.

He'd learned from Lilah. Big time.

"Look around, Zeke. Your parents have plenty of friends. I don't think they miss the Fairchilds nearly as much as you miss Lilah."

"That's not what I meant. I got over Lilah a long time ago, but losing you, losing our friendship, Mollie, that's not something I could ever get over."

It had been hard enough losing Patrick. In the years since his friend's death, Mollie had come to mean as much—if not more—to Zeke. Seeming to read his mind, her expression softened. She stepped closer and placed a hand on his arm, her touch offering an understanding and absolution Zeke wasn't sure he deserved.

"We're friends, Zeke," she said, and he couldn't resist taking her hand in his own and holding on to the promise of everything she was willing to offer. "Nothing could change that."

He'd believed that once, too. "I know you think that—"

Annoyed, she snatched her hand away. "I don't need you to tell me what I think or how I should feel. And I don't need you to apologize for kissing me because I *wanted* you to kiss me, Zeke!"

A bright blaze of color nearly obscured the freckles on her cheeks despite the bold words. But she'd always been braver than he or Patrick—or even Mollie herself—gave her credit for being. Bold and brave enough to state what she wanted and hold her head high as she demanded, "So the real question is, what do *you* want?"

There was no question, no doubt as to what Zeke wanted. He wanted to kiss Mollie and more—much more. He wanted to pull her into his arms, the same way he had in the woods behind her house, and kiss her until she—no, until *he* was begging for more.

But the desire rushing through his veins and the blood pounding in his ears wasn't enough to drown out the echo of guilt. His jaw clenched tight, he ground out, "This isn't about doing what I want. It's about doing what's right."

"And, of course, you get to be the one to decide that."

Zeke swore beneath his breath. "Do you think this is easy for me? I've spent too many years protecting you to stop now, even if that means protecting you from—"

"Protecting me from what?" When he didn't answer her demand, she seemed to come to her own conclusion.

The fire in her eyes flamed brighter than her hair as her voice rose. "From myself? Is that what you think? That I'm not smart enough—not *woman* enough—to know my own mind? You really *don't* know me, Zeke, if that's how little you think of me!"

That wasn't what he thought at all, and as Mollie stormed off, Zeke called himself every name in the book for not having the courage to admit the truth he'd feared from the moment he heard Patrick was killed. That his friend's silence and withdrawal on his last visit home were signs of something serious. That the soldier had been exhibiting classic signs of depression, and Zeke had missed it. Missed it not only as a doctor but as a friend.

If he'd pressed Patrick harder, if he hadn't been caught up in the drama around the upcoming wedding and Lilah's suddenly cold feet... If he'd paid more attention to what was right in front of him, his friend might still be alive.

Ready to tear her own hair out, Mollie seriously thought she might be the one in need of a fire extinguisher as she stormed away from Zeke. With her fair skin, she had no doubt her face was going up in flames, and she only hoped the other guests gathered at the barbecue might attribute it to the afternoon heat.

What would it take to get Zeke to see that she'd grown up? For him to stop treating her like a kid and to treat her like a woman? Despite her anger, she couldn't help feeling exactly like a child, storming off in a snit when she didn't get her way.

I wanted you to kiss me, Zeke. What do you want?

Mollie held back a groan as she stopped at one of the large coolers near the picnic tables. She stuck her arm elbow-deep into the icy water as she reached for a can of soda and imagined plunging her whole head in.

Had she really been so stupid as to say that? To ask that?

She couldn't stay mad at Zeke forever and needed to find a way to get over her embarrassment and humiliation, but like every other emotion she had when it came to Zeke Harper...easier said than done.

"Hey, Mollie," Matt Fielding greeted her as he bent down to grab a drink of his own. "Everything okay with you and Zeke?"

Though Mollie didn't know Matt well, he, like all former soldiers, had a place in her heart. Add in the smile the man had put on Claire's face and the fact that he'd recently adopted Hank, an older three-legged dog from Furever Paws that too many people had passed over, and Mollie had even more reason to be grateful to the man. But that didn't necessarily mean that she wanted to spill her guts to him. "Sure. Everything's great. How about you and Claire?"

Matt glanced across the yard with a smile as his gaze landed on his fiancée. With her shoulder-length blond hair caught back in a headband and a smile on her face as she spoke with Zeke's mother, Claire looked as lovely and as happy as ever. "She's perfect," he vowed, a hint of awe filling his deep voice.

"Glad to hear it." And she was. Glad and only a tiny bit eaten alive with envy at the way the high school sweethearts had reunited.

"Zeke tells me you came up with a potential therapy dog for Bobby Doyle."

Feeling like he was giving her too much credit, Mollie argued, "It was Zeke's idea. He's really hoping it might help."

"Well, you know Zeke better than anyone. Helping people is who he is."

Matt was right about that. Which was what made it so hard to stay angry at him. After filling Matt in on Charlie's progress, she said, "I really think Charlie could do Bobby a world of good. Of course, he'd have to continue training her. It can take eighteen months for a dog to actually be certified as a therapy dog."

"Some things don't require any training. Sometimes it's enough for a dog just to be a dog."

Mollie nodded, the lingering shadows in Matt's gaze reminders of how much he'd overcome and how much having a dog like Hank had helped. "There's a reason why they're called man's best friend."

"Speaking of best friends..." Matt tipped his head in Zeke's direction, and Mollie barely held back a groan.

"Pretty sure we were talking about dogs."

"Yeah, well, when are you gonna let that one out of the doghouse?"

"I'm not—"

"You're pissed," the ex-soldier chuckled softly. "Doesn't take a psychologist to see that."

"Zeke is my best friend, but he can be so—" *Dense. Blind. Stubborn.* "—frustrating sometimes," Mollie concluded.

"Yep," Matt agreed after taking a long swig from the bright red aluminum can. "But you gotta give the guy a break." With a sidelong glance, he added, "It's not like he knows you're in love with him."

Mollie choked on her own swallow of soda, coughing loudly enough to gain the attention of the other guests—and Zeke, who was standing a few yards away talking to Dan Sutton. Mollie focused on resettling her breathing before he rushed over to perform the Heimlich maneuver.

She didn't want to stereotype, but this somewhat stoic, tough former army corporal didn't exactly scream someone in touch with his emotional side. And if Matt had figured out how she felt about Zeke... Not to mention how she'd practically begged him to kiss her... Mollie swallowed.

Maybe her parents had the right idea. Maybe she would start wearing animal fur and go live in the wild. Anywhere that she wouldn't have to face another living soul.

Pathetic crush... Pity date...

"We're friends," she argued, but that, too, sounded way too pathetic and pitiful.

"Uh-huh. He told me he offered to try to set you up on a date. We went through just about every single guy in town, and Zeke couldn't come up with anyone."

"The whole town, and the two of you couldn't come up with one guy who'd go out with me? That's, wow..." Mortified, Mollie shook her head. "Claire told me you were a mechanic in the army, but are you sure you weren't secretly charged with interrogating people? Because, honestly, I would tell you just about anything right now if it would make you stop."

"He couldn't come up with anyone," Matt repeated, "because he thought that none of the guys were good enough for you. Doesn't that tell you something?"

"That Zeke takes looking out for his best friend's baby sister very seriously? That he doesn't want to see me with the wrong kind of guy?" Wasn't that what Zeke had said?

"Maybe." Matt said. "Or maybe he doesn't want to see you with another guy at all."

Chapter Nine

"Mollie! Over here!"

Mollie glanced across the crowded coffee shop to see Rebekah Taylor waving at her. After making her way between the full tables with her morning mocha latte in hand, Mollie slipped into the seat the new shelter director had saved for her.

"It always amazes me how busy this place is," the dark-haired woman said as she glanced around with an assessing eye.

"Well, Whole Bean kind of has the market on the caffeinated crowd. Spring Forest doesn't exactly have a coffee shop on every corner."

"This must be a prime location for networking. I bet if you sit here long enough, you'll see just about everyone in town."

"I suppose." Mollie had already done a visual sweep of the shop for the one person she *didn't* want to see.

Most days Zeke would grab a coffee before he headed into Raleigh, but by now, he would already be at the office. Not that Mollie was purposefully avoiding him. She was just...

Purposefully avoiding him.

She wouldn't be able to keep her distance forever. As angry as she was, she already missed him. Over a week had passed since the barbecue, and she'd picked up the phone more than once to update him on Charlie's training. But each time she'd hung up without making the call.

First Josh and then Matt... Both men seemed to see something more than friendship or big-brotherly concern in Zeke's actions. Their comments were enough to make Mollie want to hope, but hope was such a dangerous thing when it came to her heart and Zeke Harper.

So instead of calling Zeke, she'd called Josh and arranged for another date that weekend. He'd suggested going with some of his friends to see a jazz band play in Raleigh, and Mollie wished she was more excited by the prospect. But whenever she tried to think about the other man, her mind was immediately hijacked by memories of Zeke's kiss.

Each time, she was assailed by a wave of guilt, although she wasn't entirely sure what made her feel worse—going on a date with Josh after kissing Zeke or kissing Zeke after going on a date with Josh.

Either way, that living-in-the-wild option was looking better and better.

"I've brought the intake paperwork on the shelter's newest rescue," Rebekah was saying. "With Furever Paws still under construction, we're hoping to find a foster quickly. I thought you might want to review her history before we head over for the introduction."

"I, um, sure." Mollie reached for the manila folder Rebekah handed over. She had to hide a bit of a smile when she caught sight of the photo clipped to the front. She wasn't sure how much "history" a four-month-old golden retriever mix could have, but she appreciated Rebekah's attention to detail.

More often than not, Mollie was working with little to no information on the dogs she evaluated. Most were strays dropped off by good Samaritans or animals pulled from the overcrowded local county shelter. Still, she flipped through the paperwork as Rebekah said, "We have a foster in mind for her, but the family has children and pets."

Something in the other woman's voice had Mollie glancing up. Rebekah gave a small headshake that set her shoulder-length curls trembling. "A *lot* of children and a *lot* of pets."

Unsure what to make of the other woman's comment, Mollie murmured, "Oh…okay."

Straightening her shoulders, Rebekah insisted, "I just want to make sure that Goldie will fit in with such a…chaotic household."

Mollie supposed a house full of kids and pets could be overwhelming to some dogs and to certain ultra-organized businesswomen like Rebekah. But the image didn't strike her as chaotic. To her it all sounded…wonderful.

As she flipped back to the front page and the goofy, floppy-eared puppy who seemed to have LET'S PLAY! written all over her cute face, Mollie had a feeling Goldie would agree. "Hopefully the family will be *just right.*"

When Rebekah frowned slightly, Mollie hurried to explain, "You know, Goldie… Goldilocks."

"Oh, right."

Feeling foolish for having to explain what was obviously a lame joke, Mollie quickly asked, "How are things going with the renovations? I know Birdie and Bunny are thrilled to have you on board."

Rebekah's smile faltered a little. "Well, *they* are…"

As the other woman's voice trailed off, Mollie asked, "Is there someone at the shelter who's not as welcoming?"

When Rebekah stayed silent, Mollie's face started to heat as she feared the other woman might have felt she was prying. She was ready to wave off the question and make some kind of inane comment about the gorgeous May weather when the other woman looked up from stirring her cappuccino.

"I probably shouldn't be saying this, but it's the Whitakers' nephew, Grant."

Though Grant Whitaker lived in Florida, he'd returned to Spring Forest several times over the past few months. Mollie had been impressed with his obvious love for his aunts, but she wasn't surprised that the marketing manager with his laid-back surfer vibe had clashed with Rebekah's type A personality.

"I know the Whitaker sisters adore him, and he's supposed to be some kind of business whiz." Rebekah's eye roll seemed to refute that possibility. "But, honestly, what kind of serious businessman wears flip-flops and thinks a T-shirt printed with Surf's Up is appropriate work attire? And if he's nearly as important as Birdie and Bunny think he is, how can he afford to miss so much work by coming up here every other week to 'check on things'?"

Mollie had always found the Whitaker sisters to be pretty good judges of character, though she did wonder a bit at their unquestioning loyalty to family. They'd stayed close to their brother Moose, Grant's father, even after he sold his share of the property and moved to Florida, leaving the family home behind. The youngest sibling, their brother Gator, had also been left a parcel of land in Spring Forest but sold out years ago and made a fortune with the reinvested money.

All of which made him sound like a man capable of advising his siblings, but he was also the one who'd let the insurance on the shelter lapse. An oversight, according to the sisters, but Mollie, Amanda and Claire weren't so sure. Maybe family ties had blinded the sisters to some of Grant's faults, as well.

Still, she pointed out, "I'm sure he just wants to know that the money brought in by last month's fund-raiser and the grant you've received are put to good use."

"I suppose," Rebekah admitted, "but it would help if he didn't watch me as if I'm planning to run off with the funds the moment he turns his back."

With her dark hair, hazel eyes and matching dimples in a heart-shaped face, Rebekah was a stunning woman. Throw in a curvy body and a sharp mind, and Mollie wondered if it wasn't something other than suspicion that kept Grant's eyes glued to her every move. Still, she swallowed the suggestion before she could make it. Who was she to think she knew anything about romance? As Zeke would quickly point out, she was clearly "mistaken."

Fortunately, Rebekah didn't seem to expect a response. With a glance at the watch on her wrist, she said, "Are you ready to head over to the shelter? I've asked Goldie's potential foster to meet us there at nine."

Glancing at the coffeepot clock hanging behind the

barista's counter, Mollie figured leaving now would give them a good twenty-seven minutes to spare, but she nodded anyway and lifted her cup. "I can take this to go."

Two hours later, Mollie's professional assessment of the young golden retriever was that she was energetic but with a low prey drive, highly treat-motivated and eager to please. Her personal opinion was that Goldie was about the cutest fluff ball she'd ever seen and she pretty much wanted to squeeze her to death. Needless to say, Mollie gave the go-ahead for Goldie to be fostered by the Nelsons.

"Thank you for the evaluation," Rebekah said as she somewhat futilely brushed at the golden fur clinging to her straight black skirt. "I'm glad Goldie has a new temporary home."

"I'm sure she'll find a permanent one soon, too, if the Nelsons don't end up adopting her themselves."

Rebekah's hands stilled. "But they already have two dogs. And a cat…and children."

"They do," Mollie agreed, but from what she'd seen, the family also had a serious case of puppy love where Goldie was concerned. Giving a single shoulder shrug, she suggested to Rebekah, "The more the merrier?"

"That's what I always say!"

Mollie turned at the sound of the bubbly voice behind her. A dark-haired woman with warm brown eyes and a friendly smile held out her hand. "Emma Alvarez. Crazy cat lady."

Laughing, Mollie shook the other woman's hand. "Mollie McFadden, crazy dog lady."

With a sigh, Rebekah said, "Well, I see that the two of you will have plenty in common. Mollie, Emma just moved to Spring Forest and is a volunteer in our cattery. Mollie is our resident dog whisperer."

"So what brought you to Spring Forest?"

The twenty-something woman lifted a shoulder in a shrug. "Oh, you know," she said vaguely. "The usual."

Unsure what that might mean, Mollie was grateful when Rebekah chimed in saying, "I'm hoping to talk Emma into volunteering as a foster, especially now that it's kitten season and we have so many pregnant moms and babies."

"And I'd love to," Emma insisted, "once I get…well, a few things worked out."

A hint of a frown shadowed the woman's sunny expression, and Mollie impulsively said, "I hope you do. Those kittens would be lucky to have you take care of them. Until then, I'm sure you'll enjoy volunteering at Furever Paws as much as I have."

"Thanks, Mollie. I'm hoping Spring Forest will be a fresh start for me."

After Emma excused herself to go check with Richard Jackson, a local veterinarian who volunteered at the rescue, Rebekah said, "Speaking of fosters, how's it going with Charlie and Chief? I've been meaning to thank you. Birdie was so happy when you decided to take both of them on."

"I'm pretty sure that was Birdie's idea all along, but honestly, having the two of them together has made fostering Chief so much easier. He's come so far in just a few weeks—which is good, since Zeke Harper has an idea for a permanent placement for Charlie."

Quickly, Mollie filled the shelter director in on Bobby Doyle and Zeke's hope that Charlie could become a companion dog for the veteran. "It's something I'd like to do more of in the future, partnering the shelter and Veterans Affairs to match up dogs with former servicemen and -women in need."

"That sounds like a great opportunity—for Charlie and for the shelter." Reaching for her phone, Rebekah tapped in some quick notes. "But…what about Chief? How's he going to handle being separated from Charlie?"

As excited as she was for the opportunity to train Charlie and to hopefully help Bobby, Mollie was concerned about poor Chief, too. "I've been working one-on-one with him to build up his confidence and also encouraging more interaction between Chief and my dog, Arti. Given enough time, I think he'll forget all about Ze—I mean, Charlie."

Fortunately, Rebekah didn't seem to notice the slip of the tongue. "Good. It will certainly be easier to adopt him out if he doesn't have to be part of a matched pair."

Mollie nodded even as she tucked her chin against her chest. Sure, Chief could learn to be an only dog, but it didn't seem fair for him to have to go through life alone. Didn't everyone deserve a soul mate? Maybe Arti could be Chief's.

And maybe, just maybe, if she tried a little harder to finally get over Zeke, Josh Sylvester could be hers.

As Zeke pulled up to Furever Paws, a sudden knot gripped his stomach. Though he and Matt believed a therapy dog might be good for Bobby, both men had agreed to wait to talk to the former soldier until they knew for sure that a dog could be found. The last thing they'd wanted was to get Bobby's hopes up.

Now, though, with the meeting with Charlie and the former army mechanic about to take place, Zeke realized the biggest hopes might well be his own. Mollie had worked so hard with the sweet, sensitive Lab, and Zeke knew Charlie would be perfect for Bobby, but would Bobby think so?

Zeke had convinced Bobby to come to the shelter. From there, it would be up to Mollie and Charlie. Zeke had to believe those two gorgeous females would work their magic on the tough army vet, but that wasn't enough to soothe the sudden attack of nerves.

Hell, he didn't know how the Whitaker sisters put up with this kind of pressure. So many animals in need of good homes but no guarantee that the right adopter would come along.

Maybe Mollie was right. Maybe he should think about adopting a dog. He could use a friend to hang out and watch television with in the evenings or to go hiking with early in the morning on the weekends or to lounge with in the backyard once the sun went down… All activities he used to do with Mollie.

He missed her. He missed the ease and comfort of their friendship, which had been replaced by an awkwardness and simmering attraction. Wasn't that why he'd insisted on maintaining a platonic friendship? Because he didn't want their relationship to change? And yet…hadn't it changed already, whether he wanted it to or not?

As Zeke climbed from his car and eyed the shelter in the late afternoon sun, he could see the progress that had been made in the past few weeks—the new roof was already in place and the area around the back staked off for the expansion that would soon be breaking ground. Hearing female voices from the side of the building, he followed the sound. His greeting died on his lips, though, as he caught sight of the Whitaker sisters huddled together.

Though the taller, older Birdie was known for her stoic, no-nonsense attitude, even Bunny's normally smiling round face was drawn into a grimace. "Do you really think we should look into selling?"

Zeke hadn't intended to eavesdrop, but he couldn't help but respond to what he'd heard. "Selling?"

Hadn't he just been thinking how emotionally draining it must be to work with the homeless animals? But at the same time, he couldn't imagine the sisters walking away from Furever Paws. This was their home, established on the property that had been left to them after their brothers sold their shares of the family estate. Zeke couldn't imagine anything shaking their commitment to the shelter. Especially after hiring the new director and the success of last month's fund-raiser.

The two women glanced up, clearly surprised by his presence. "Oh, Zeke," Bunny said softly. "We didn't even see you there."

"Sorry, I don't mean to pry but—"

"No, it's all right," Birdie said as she managed a slight smile. "We've received another offer on some of the acreage we inherited when our parents died. We've held on to it since then…"

"But with the damage done to the shelter, we've been considering whether or not we should sell," Bunny finished.

"I know there's still a lot of work to be done, but the money brought in by the fund-raiser and the grant should be a big help, right?" Zeke asked.

"We weren't looking to sell the land," Bunny admitted, "but Gator says…" Her voice trailed off as the two women exchanged yet another glance. "He feels so bad about everything that's happened here after the insurance fell through, and he wants to help out. He's the one who found the buyer for the land and has promised to handle the details so we wouldn't need to be involved."

"He does know far more about this type of thing than we do," Birdie admitted.

Treading carefully, he said, "I'm sure Gator has plenty of experience, but maybe you could have Dan Sutton review the paperwork."

The Spring Forest lawyer was known for being fair and for looking out for the local residents. Zeke wouldn't be surprised if the man offered his services at a reduced fee.

"That's a good idea." Birdie nodded. "It's a big decision and not one to make lightly."

Glad to see the frowns easing from the sisters' faces, Zeke said, "It's always best to have all the information up front and to consider all the ramifications before making a decision."

"Thank you, Zeke." Brushing her hands against the front of her khaki slacks, as if eager to wipe away her worries, Birdie said, "Now, when is Mr. Doyle arriving?"

As the talk turned to Bobby and all of their hopes that Charlie could work her canine magic on the battle-scarred veteran, the three of them made their way into the shelter. A cacophony of sounds assaulted Zeke as he stepped inside the reception area, the barks and play growls of dogs, the constant and almost questioning meow of a talkative cat—heck, he was pretty sure he even heard the distant squawk of a parrot—all mixed in with human voices, the ringing of a phone and the constant hum of a printer.

A young family in one corner knelt down to play with a rambunctious beagle puppy in a tug of war with its own leash under the amused yet watchful eye of a

Furever Paws adoption coordinator. Another woman stood behind the reception desk, talking on the phone, while Rebekah Taylor was in a serious discussion with Richard Jackson, the semi-retired veterinarian who so tirelessly volunteered his services.

The organized chaos was all a bit much, and Zeke hoped Bobby wouldn't be instantly overwhelmed. He was about to suggest that they move the meet and greet to an outdoor area when Dr. Jackson, or Doc J, as he was more commonly known, broke away from Rebekah.

Walking over to Zeke, the tall older man greeted him with a handshake. "Zeke, good to see you!" His smile was a bright contrast with his brown skin. "How are your parents doing? Sorry I missed the barbecue the other day. My daughter, Lauren, had us booked for a father-daughter golf outing."

"They're doing well. The barbecue might have been the first of the summer, but I doubt it will be the last."

After a few minutes of small talk, Doc J took Zeke's arm and moved them farther away from the Whitaker sisters and the potential adopters. Glancing over his shoulder, the veterinarian said, "I couldn't help noticing that you were talking with Birdie and Bunny."

Though the Whitaker sisters weren't his patients, Zeke took confidentiality seriously in all parts of his life. But he knew the sisters considered Doc J to be a good friend, so brushing him off wasn't an option. "They're worried about the shelter," he admitted, figuring that wasn't any revelation to the veterinarian. Not giving away any state secrets there.

Doc J sighed. "They've had a lot on their minds recently, that's for sure." His dark eyes, still sharp despite the lines feathering out from the corners, focused on the two women. "First the tornado, then the mess with the insurance and now this offer to buy some of the land…"

Zeke's shoulders loosened bit. "Sounds like you know as much I do. I suggested that they talk to Dan Sutton to get a second opinion on the offer."

The doc's salt-and-pepper eyebrows rose. "How'd they take that?"

Zeke shrugged as he tapped a red rubber ball bouncing his way with the tip of his tennis shoe. The beagle racing toward him, tail and ears streaming out behind, nearly tipped tail over teakettle as it skidded to a stop on the concrete floor and charged the other way after the elusive toy. "They seemed to think it was a good idea. Hard to say if they'll follow through with it, though."

"Oh, I'll make sure they do," Doc J vowed. "They can be so—so stubborn sometimes when it comes to asking for help."

Zeke gave half a laugh. How well he recognized those words, that frustration, even the look on the other man's face that spoke of something more than friendship… Glancing over, Zeke couldn't tell which of the two very different women had caught the older man's eye.

At least he didn't have that problem.

He knew perfectly well what woman held his interest.

He just didn't know what the hell to do about it.

Chapter Ten

Mollie didn't realize she'd been holding her breath until it all escaped in a rush as Bobby Doyle slowly bent down to greet Charlie. Zeke had arranged for the former soldier to meet the young pup in the small grassy area beside the shelter. The two of them exchanged a quick glance, and she knew Zeke was as nervous and hopeful about this introduction as she was.

Though she'd talked Bobby up to Charlie on the ride over, assuring the dog that Bobby would take one look and fall in love with her, Mollie knew a perfect match wasn't always so easy to find.

"Don't you worry, baby girl," she'd told Charlie. "You just be yourself and Bobby's bound to love you."

Mollie had meant the words as an encouragement to the dog, but an echo of truth resounded through the words. *Be yourself...*

She couldn't help thinking of her first date with Josh.

Of the fancy hair and makeup, the dress and heels she'd worn. Sure, her friends had insisted they were only bringing out her natural beauty, but the real Mollie was all about ponytails and lip balm, faded T-shirts and comfy jeans.

Maybe she needed to take her own advice on her upcoming date with Josh. It certainly seemed to be working for Charlie. The minute Bobby knelt down, the sensitive Lab placed a paw on the former soldier's knee. Both seemed to bow their heads in a moment of silent communication. For Mollie, it was one of the most touching, emotional scenes she'd ever witnessed. She'd *never* been a sucker for weddings, but this...

Blinking back the ache of tears, she started when Zeke took her hand. As her gaze met his, Mollie saw the understanding reflected there. He knew her so well and—

Oh, crap... She was never getting over him, was she?

Not for Josh Sylvester or, she feared, any other man on the face of the earth.

"She's—" Bobby cleared his throat. "She's pretty special, isn't she?"

His eyes still locked on Mollie, Zeke agreed, "Yes, she is."

He must have come to the shelter straight from his office in Raleigh. Though he'd loosened the maroon tie around his neck and rolled the sleeves of the navy dress shirt up his leanly muscled forearms, he still looked so sophisticated and so handsome. But it was the emotion in his hazel eyes that made it impossible to pull her gaze away. As the moment of connection strengthened and grew, Charlie finally gave a sudden bark, as if to remind her distracted human why they were there in the first place.

Pulling her hand from Zeke's, Mollie focused on Bobby. A look of pure puppy love softened the former soldier's rough-hewn features as he rubbed his work-scarred hands over the dog's soft ears.

"I tend to say this about all the dogs I've fostered and trained, but you're right. Charlie is special. Don't let her good looks fool you into underestimating her. She's one smart pup."

"Yeah? What kind of tricks can she do?"

Biting the inside of her cheek, she glanced over at Zeke, who gave a nod of encouragement. She had to tread carefully during this next part. From what she and Zeke had learned from Matt, Bobby had yet to admit he was having trouble adjusting to civilian life.

"Well…" Mollie gave a quick laugh. "I have to admit, I'm not much of a morning person, but the minute my alarm goes off, Charlie is by my bedside, ready for a walk, her leash in her mouth."

"Really?" Bobby's eyes lit up. "You can do that?" he asked the dog who responded with an enthusiastic lick to the man's face.

"Oh, she can do that." No real training had been required to get the young dog up and at 'em at the crack of dawn. And with the natural instincts of a retriever, teaching Charlie to grab her leash hadn't taken long, either. Conditioning that behavior to coincide with the sound of the alarm had been the biggest challenge, but they'd accomplished it.

"I suppose it wouldn't hurt for me to get out and moving. I used to love hitting the trails around here, but I haven't done that since… Well, it's been a while."

Mollie tried to hide her excitement. That was the idea. Not just as a way to encourage Bobby to give

Charlie the exercise and attention an active dog needed, but also as a motivation for Bobby to stay busy.

"Of course, she already knows sit and come. Stay is a tough one for her, and I never suggest owners let their dogs off leash unless they are in a secure area. She loves her treats and her b-a-l-l." She spelled out the favorite word to keep Charlie from getting too excited, but judging by the way the Lab's ears perked up, she may well have already figured that out.

"And studies have shown that owning a dog can lower blood pressure and even help minimize risks of heart attack and stroke," Zeke chimed in. "Not to mention the emotional benefits like helping with stress and anxiety."

At that, Bobby frowned and pushed to his feet. His face turned red as he eyed Zeke and Mollie. "Don't tell me this is some kind of—doggie intervention. I told you I don't need help!"

"No, it's not! It's—" Panicked, and worried that Bobby was about to walk out on all three of them, Charlie included, Mollie looked to Zeke for help.

But Zeke took the other man's outburst in stride. His voice calm and controlled, he said, "This is just you checking out a dog and seeing if she'll be a good fit for your family. It doesn't have to be anything more than that."

For a long moment, Bobby stood silent and still... until Charlie broke the standoff. Nudging his arm with her head, she didn't give him much choice but to start petting her again. "But it could be," he murmured quietly as he dug his fingers into the thick ruff of fur around Charlie's neck. "That's what you're saying, isn't it?" Keeping his gaze on the dog as he knelt back down, Bobby quietly asked, "What would she be able to do to help me?"

Trusting in Charlie and the training they'd done, Mollie explained how the dog could be taught to pick up on cues that Bobby was exhibiting signs of depression, night terrors or slipping into a flashback. "You really think she could do all that?" he asked.

"I know she can," Mollie said confidently. "We'll have to work together to come up with the right reward system to mark the behavior you want from Charlie. The behavior could be anything from curling up beside you, nudging your arm to encourage you to pet her, or licking your face—whatever helps."

Right on cue, Charlie lifted her head and swiped at Bobby's chin with her tongue, making the humans laugh and breaking some of the tension.

"So, what do you think?" Zeke asked after a few more minutes letting man and dog bond.

Bobby gave a smile that reached his eyes. "I think this girl has found herself a home."

The trail of dust behind Bobby's classic pickup had barely settled before Mollie threw her arms around Zeke's neck. Caught off guard, he stumbled slightly before getting his bearings and bracketing his hands at her waist.

"You did it, Zeke!" Her smile was as bright as the sky overhead as she gazed up at him. "Did you see how happy Bobby looked? I thought he was going to buy half the dog toys in the gift shop."

"Charlie's going to be one spoiled pup."

"All thanks to you."

Suddenly, Zeke was taken back to the day they'd rescued Shadow, when Mollie had looked at him with such pride and adoration even though, really, it had been Mollie. It had always been Mollie.

He wasn't about to dim her enthusiasm by pointing out that Bobby still had a long way to go in dealing with his PTSD. The former soldier had taken the first step toward getting help, and Zeke was going to focus on that and the light shining in Mollie's eyes for now. He drew in a deep breath. He hadn't been able to help Patrick, but he could still help Bobby and others like him.

Still he argued, "You're giving me too much credit. You're the one who's been working so hard with Charlie."

She shrugged off the praise. "Charlie made it easy. She's a natural."

Her smile wavered a bit. Even though she'd only fostered the sweet Lab for a few weeks, Zeke knew Mollie would miss her. Hoping to distract her, he asked, "Hey, how did the photos turn out?"

"I almost forgot!" Before Bobby had completed the adoption paperwork, she'd ask Bunny to take some shots of the two of them with Bobby and Charlie. Stepping back, she pulled her phone from her back pocket.

"Oh, that is so cute!" she exclaimed over an image of Charlie snuggled up to Bobby's chest. A look of sheer adoration filled her dark puppy eyes. Of course, Bobby looked almost as smitten as—as Zeke did in the very next photo. Only he wasn't looking at the dog. Instead the image had been snapped right as Mollie tipped her head back in laughter and Zeke... He'd been caught gazing at her with an expression on his face that he'd never seen before.

He reached for the phone, his hand covering the backs of her fingers. His thumb hovered over the screen.

He didn't know if he wanted to delete the evidence or send the photo to his own phone.

Seeming to think he was having trouble with the late afternoon glare, Mollie tilted the cell in his direction. A hint of pink touched her cheeks as she glanced at him from the corner of her eye. A faint breeze stirred the curls against the side of her neck and carried a sun-warmed wildflower scent straight to his senses. "Can you see it?"

He had to clear his throat before he could answer, his voice dropping an octave as he admitted, "I can see it."

And now that he had, he didn't know how he had been so blind for so long. He was falling for his best friend. As soon as the thought crossed his mind, Zeke rejected it. He'd been through love's crazy roller coaster ride of highs and lows, not to mention the loops that turned his well-ordered life upside down, and he wanted no part of it.

His fingers tensed against hers, and Mollie's thumb jerked. "Oops." She laughed a bit shakily as she ended up opening another album file to reveal a photo that had to be over two years old, although he'd never seen it before.

Patrick stared back at him from the screen, a wry smile on his handsome face as he posed with an arm around Mollie. His hair was cut military short, his bearing that of a soldier even though he wore a faded pair of jeans and a Tar Heels T-shirt.

"That's the last picture I have of him," Mollie said softly. "It was taken on his final trip home."

The revelation had Zeke drawing the phone closer. He stared harder at the photo, as if the two-dimensional image might reveal all the secrets his living, breathing friend had kept to himself. Zeke took in the decked-out Christmas tree in the background, towering well above his friend's six-foot frame. Was it only Zeke's imagination or did the bright lights from the tree only make the shadows in his friend's gaze that much more obvious? The cheery holiday trappings were such a contrast to Patrick's somber, troubled mood during that last visit. Only—

"Patrick's last visit was in March," Zeke said. He was sure of it, as Lilah had called the wedding off only a few weeks later. And then a month later Patrick had been killed.

"Yes, it was."

He turned the screen toward Mollie. "So, what's with the Christmas tree?"

"Oh, that." Mollie gave a little laugh. "Patrick had told my parents he'd be home for the holidays. But his leave kept getting pushed back for one reason or another, and by the time he finally made it back, it was already March. So Santa came a bit late to the McFadden house that year."

"Seriously? Your family waited three months to celebrate Christmas? I mean, I get waiting for Patrick to get home for him to open his presents, but you—Mollie, you were already here."

"It didn't matter," she insisted as she pulled her hand away from his and pocketed the phone. Her head ducked toward her chin. "Christmas wasn't Christmas without Patrick, anyway."

Zeke heard the words Mollie spoke but he also listened to everything she didn't say. *It didn't matter* just as easily could have been *I didn't matter.*

"It's no big deal," said the girl who started decorating for the holidays the second the Thanksgiving dishes were washed and put away. The girl who always remembered her friends' birthdays, who never failed to put up some kind of decoration to mark seasonal events—including dressing up Arti in costumes ranging from wings and a bow and arrow for Valentine's Day to a turkey headdress for Thanksgiving.

"Mollie…" Zeke's gut clenched. He didn't blame the McFaddens for the extreme pride they had in their first-born son. He felt the same way when he thought of his friend. Patrick was a true hero. A soldier who had lived and died for his country. Patrick deserved to have his memory honored.

But Zeke would never understand why the McFaddens put more time and effort and energy into mourning the son who had died than into appreciating their daughter, who was still very much alive.

Mollie wasn't a soldier, but she fought for the homeless and helpless animals who needed her. She was strong and brave and beautiful… How could her parents not see how smart and caring and accomplished she was?

How had *he* not seen that?

As hard as it was to admit, Zeke suddenly realized he'd done his own share of devaluing her efforts. Had he really thought she wouldn't be able to handle two new foster dogs when her gift with animals was beyond anything he'd ever witnessed? Had he really believed she wouldn't be able to fix up the house when she'd spent her childhood proving to him and to Patrick that she could do anything they could? Had he really spent so much time with her since Patrick's death because Mollie needed him…or was it because he needed Mollie?

"Don't." She held out a hand, her blue-green eyes suspiciously bright. "I don't need you to feel sorry for me."

He gently caught her wrist and brought her hand to his mouth. "Why would I," he whispered as he brushed his lips against her palm, "when you are the strongest, bravest, most beautiful woman I know?"

"And don't say things like that, either," she whispered. Despite her words, she curled her fingers against his jaw, her touch feather-light.

"Why not?"

Carefully withdrawing her hand from his, she murmured, "Because you make me want to believe that you mean them."

"I meant every word."

"You're a good friend, Zeke. But when you say things like that…you make me want more than just friendship."

"Mollie…" Zeke swallowed hard and opened his mouth. It was his turn now to warn her not to say things that made him want. But the words wouldn't come. And before he could try again she had turned and walked away.

In the days following Charlie's adoption, Mollie made an effort to spend even more time with Arti and Chief for the dogs' sake and for her own. Both of them had noticed Charlie's absence when she arrived home without their friend. Arti, who was used to the coming and going of the dogs Mollie fostered or trained in-home, settled down quickly, but Chief had broken her heart a little, lying by the front door waiting for the other dog's return.

She'd taken both dogs out for a run and then for a play session every morning, and Chief seemed to gradually bounce back, chasing and wrestling Arti on the lush green grass. He'd come so far since she first saw him huddled in the corner in his kennel. She knew he was almost ready for adoption but wasn't sure she was ready to let him go.

The shy dog had worked his way into her heart just like she knew he would, and having him around, seeing Chief and Arti together, made Mollie feel a little less lonely. She missed Zeke. She missed his easy smile. His calm logic in the face of her sometimes overboard rush to action. She missed his friendship and had no one but herself to blame for the distance between them on multiple levels. After all, she was the one who'd been avoiding him, too embarrassed by the too-revealing comments that bypassed her brain and went straight out her mouth whenever they were together.

First practically begging him to kiss her and then telling him she wanted more. Mollie groaned and wanted to hide her heated face in her hands every time she thought about it.

You are the strongest, bravest, most beautiful woman I know.

Not that strong and not that brave.

Mollie lips quirked a little in a self-deprecating smile. Maybe she'd give him one out of the three.

Saturday morning, she received a text from a client who had to cancel her afternoon appointment. Mollie had rescheduled the destructive poodle's training session for the following week, wondering how many shoes, pillows and sofas the brilliant but bored dog would leave in her wake in the meantime.

With nothing else planned until her date with Josh that evening, Mollie decided to tackle her most pressing home improvement project. A few nights earlier, she'd seen an aging shutter on an upper story window listing to the side, barely hanging on by a hinge.

A voice in her head that sounded a lot like her brother's told her she should call Zeke but…no. She was too embarrassed to face him yet. After a trip to the shed in the backyard, she stuck a few screwdrivers into her belt loops, her makeshift version of a tool belt, and awkwardly banged her way through the side gate with an unwieldy extension ladder.

She'd just reached the second-story shutter when she heard a familiar snuffling sound behind her. For a panicked instant, she worried one of her dogs had somehow gotten out. But when she glanced over her shoulder, the dog she saw wasn't one of hers. Even so, her hands tightened on the rung of the ladder at the sight of the small, scruffy gray terrier nosing along the edge of her property.

She'd seen the dog a few months ago, but hadn't been able to coax him close enough to catch. "Poor puppy," she murmured, seeing how much thinner and stragglier the stray looked since the last time she'd seen him.

The dog didn't seem to notice her presence as he cautiously padded closer to the open gate. If curiosity would only bring him into the backyard, she could latch the gate and safely lock the illusive dog inside.

The terrier was almost, almost inside the gate when he froze and looked back, ears twitching. A moment later, Mollie heard the sound the little dog had obviously picked up on first. The crunch of tires along the drive and the low rumble of an engine.

"Don't run…don't run," she whispered, but at the slam of a car door, instinct had him rushing toward the closest safe place. The small dog was little more than a gray blur, darting into the crawl space beneath the side of the house.

Hoping she could coax the dog back out, Mollie hurried down the ladder and ducked down to peer through the small gap in the latticed fascia. With the dog's ashy coloring, she couldn't even see him amid the shadows. Trying for a better angle, she lay down flat on the sun-warmed grass. But for a small dog to survive on its own for so long, it had to be smart, fast…and very good at hiding. Maybe some food might lure the hungry terrier out, but as she pushed into a sitting position to head to the kitchen, she heard Zeke call out her name.

"Mollie! Oh, my God, Mollie."

"Hey—"

She was about to explain about the dog when Zeke dropped to his knees beside her. He caught her shoulders in his hands and completely stole her breath with the fierce intensity written across his handsome features. "Don't move," he commanded.

Her heart racing like a NASCAR engine roaring along the Charlotte Motor Speedway, she couldn't have lifted a finger to save her life as he lowered her back to the ground.

His broad shoulders blocked out the sun, but Mollie still felt on fire as he ran his hands over her, starting with her neck and working his way down. As she gazed up at him, it took her brain a few minutes to catch on to the fact that his movements were brisk and efficient, professional, rather than the long, lingering caresses of a lover. Her body, however, didn't care.

"Zeke—" she started to protest.

"Stay still," he insisted. "Any dizziness? Shortness of breath? Are you feeling any pain?"

Yes, yes and yes…

Simply being so close to him, inhaling his woodsy aftershave combined with the summer grasses, made her head spin. His warm, strong hands moving down the bare skin of her leg, from her thigh all the way down to her ankle, had her gasping for air. And the desire building inside her made her ache to feel his mouth pressed to her own...

But if Zeke had any thought of putting his lips on hers, it would be only to give her mouth-to-mouth resuscitation.

As he started on her other leg, his touch moving from her calf, to her knee, to the inside of her thigh, Mollie jerked in reaction, nearly planting her tennis shoe straight in the middle of his chest as she scrambled out of reach. "Cut it out, Zeke. I'm fine!"

She pushed to her feet on shaky legs, determined not to let him know how such an impersonal examination had affected her. She crossed her arms over her stomach when what she really wanted to do was cover her breasts and hide her body's reaction to his touch. She felt naked, exposed and thoroughly embarrassed by how easily he could turn her on...and still feel nothing in return.

"You were lying on the ground." Confusion and a good dose of fear mixed in his hazel eyes as he stared up at her. Slowly climbing to his feet, he ran a hand over his face. "Dammit, Mollie, I thought you'd fallen off the ladder. It would be just like you to—"

His words cut off, but she'd hear them often enough to know how the refrain ended. "To what?" she challenged. "Do something stupid? 'That Mollie, always getting in over her head! She never looks before she leaps!'"

Fury pounded in her chest even though the criticisms

were spot-on. She certainly hadn't looked before jumping head over heels in love with Zeke Harper, and where had that gotten her?

She broke off with one of her brother's favorite curses, barely noticing Zeke's flinch, as she caught sight of streak of gray from the corner of her eye. She turned in time to see the flash of a ragged tail disappear down the long driveway and out of sight.

"Mollie, what on earth—" Zeke called after her as she took off at a sprint.

"The dog, Zeke!" Mollie yelled back as she ran, but by the time she reached the front of her property, the little terrier was long gone and so was her hope of catching him. Sucking in a breath, she looked down one side of the road and then the other but saw no sight of him.

"What dog?" Zeke demanded as he caught up behind her.

"The stray that's been spotted around town. He was hiding beneath the house. That's why I was on the ground—to try to coax him out. That was my one chance at rescuing him until you—" So furious with him, with herself, she shook her head in disgust as she brushed past him.

"Until I what, Mollie? Do you know what I thought— what I *felt*—seeing you lying on the ground like that? Thinking that you were hurt? That you were—"

As Mollie turned back, she got her first good look at Zeke. With his hands on his knees and his chest heaving, he looked like he'd run five miles rather than the dozen yards down her drive. "Zeke—"

Closing his eyes, he ground out, "I'll help you catch the damn dog, Mollie. Just give me a second, would you?"

A sharp retort pricked the tip of her tongue. How

many times would she have snapped back that she didn't need his help?

You know Zeke better than anyone. Helping people is who he is.

Matt's words tugged at her conscience. Maybe she didn't need his help. But Zeke needed to help, and maybe, just maybe, what he needed most from her was for her to let him.

Loose gravel crunched beneath her sneaks as she walked over to him. His eyes opened as she placed a hand on his arm, and her chest tightened at the lingering worry and fear she saw written in his gorgeous hazel eyes. "Zeke, you know I'm fine, right? I didn't fall off the ladder."

"When I saw you—when I thought—" He released another long, ragged breath as he pulled her into his embrace. His arms wrapped so tight around her waist that Mollie didn't think he'd ever let go. Didn't ever want him to let go. "I don't know what I'd do if I lost you, too, Moll."

Tears burned the back of her throat. "You won't," she vowed, her voice rough with the ache of their shared loss. "You can't." Determined not to let sorrow cloud her best memories—ones of the three of them together— she forced a smile into her words. "Remember all those times you and Patrick tried to ditch me while we were growing up? Never worked, did it?" Leaning far enough back to look up at him, she vowed, "You're stuck with me, Zeke Harper."

Reaching up a still-trembling hand, he brushed a strand of hair back from her face. Her skin burned as his fingertips lingered on her cheek, and Mollie wouldn't have been surprised if his touch left a new trail of freckles in its wake.

"The little sister I never wanted." He murmured the oft-repeated phrase and yet somehow the words sounded...different.

Not a light tease but weighted with the awareness that the words were no longer true. She wasn't little, she wasn't his sister and, if she could believe the desire in his gaze, Zeke did, indeed, want her.

She stood close enough to feel the heat of his body and to breathe in the scent of his skin, but she craved so much more. A slow shudder slid down her spine as he ran his fingers through her hair, and Mollie had to know. "Why were you sorry you kissed me?"

His eyes darkened like the North Carolina woods after a drenching rain, and Mollie knew if she wasn't careful, she could lose herself in their mysterious depths forever. "I wasn't sorry."

"You apologized. You said it was a mistake," she reminded him, feeling the flush of humiliation rising in her cheeks.

"I was apologizing for the way I kissed you."

As far as Mollie was concerned, the amazing, soul-stealing kiss was nothing to apologize for. "I don't understand."

"I practically attacked you." This time, embarrassed color flushed his cheekbones, but Zeke being Zeke, he held her gaze despite his discomfort. "That's not what a first kiss should be, but the second I touched you, I just—went a little crazy."

Zeke was the most controlled person Mollie knew. The idea that she could make him lose that control, even for a moment, was as heady and powerful as that first kiss. "Crazy can be good."

He gave a low groan. "Mollie, you know this will only complicate things."

Ignoring his warning, she rose up on tiptoe. Still not tall enough to reach his mouth, she brushed her lips against his chin. The slight friction of stubble against her skin had Mollie going weak in the knees. "I want to kiss you again. What could be simpler than that?"

"I'm not going to want to stop at kissing." The raw intensity of the words threatened to turn her muscles to jelly. "And that's where things get complicated."

"I won't want you to stop, either." Mollie had never been so bold or acted so recklessly, only the thought of making love with Zeke didn't feel reckless; it felt right. "So, now we're back to simple."

Cursing beneath his breath, he closed his eyes as he bent to press his forehead against hers. "I swear, Mollie, you are so—"

"What?" she whispered.

"Stubborn. Hardheaded. Frustrating."

Not exactly flowery praise, but considering she'd thought almost the same about Zeke the day of the picnic when she'd been dying to kiss him, Mollie decided not to hold a grudge. Especially not when he lowered his head to claim her lips.

As if trying to make up for whatever he felt that previous kiss lacked, this one was sweet yet seductive. Tempting yet tender. Endless and yet over far too soon. All a first kiss should be...

When Zeke finally lifted his head, his breathing was ragged. Boneless and aching, she could feel his struggle for control in the rock-hard muscles beneath her hands, see it in the battle in his green-gold eyes. "Mollie." His throat worked as he swallowed. "This— you and me—this could change everything."

Trying for a casual shrug as she stepped out of his embrace, she said, "It wouldn't have to."

He pinned her with an intense look that silenced her before she could suggest anything as foolish as friends with benefits. "I think it would be...wise to take things slow."

Slow? Slow! It had taken him twenty flipping years to kiss her! At this rate, she'd die of sexual starvation before he ever attempted second base. "And you think I'm frustrating," she muttered, kicking at a loose rock along the path.

He chuckled at that, relaxing some of the tension pulling so tightly between them and easing Mollie's worries. The shared laughter, so much a part of their relationship, proved as nothing else could that no matter what changed between them, they would always be friends.

"Don't forget hardheaded."

"And stubborn," Mollie added with a cheeky lift of her chin. All of which was true. She didn't give up, and now that Zeke had kissed her, now that he'd admitted he wanted her, she had even more reason to hold on to the hope that had lived in her heart for so long.

"All right, we'll take things slow, but first I have a favor to ask." She had to chuckle a little at the wary look in his eyes even as heat pooled in her belly. What exactly was he imagining her asking of him? Licking her lips, she watched his gaze drop to her mouth. "I was wondering if you would, um, help me hang that shutter?"

Chapter Eleven

Once Mollie explained why she'd gone up on the ladder in the first place, Zeke had made his own inspection of all of the shutters. Years of exposure to rain and sun and the recent tornado had done their damage. "No sense in rehanging one if the rest are all about to come loose," he'd determined.

He'd offered to accompany her to the home improvement store. Between Mollie's typical stubbornness and her not-so-typical but recent tendency to avoid him, he half expected her to refuse. She'd surprised him by agreeing, though she insisted her vehicle was better suited for hauling the necessary woodwork.

Zeke didn't care that she wanted to drive. Hell, he would have walked barefoot if that's what she asked him to do. Crazy to be looking forward to a trip to the huge hardware store, but as he buckled in and caught Mollie's wildflower-fresh scent mixing with the warm summer air streaming through the windows, he knew the destination had nothing to do with the anticipation humming along his nerve endings.

It was Mollie. Spending time with her. Hanging out like they used to.

But he wasn't used to sneaking glances from the corner of his eye at the wild curls she'd caught up in a high ponytail, revealing the elegant length of her neck and the delicate curve of her ear. He took in her feminine profile, following the slope of her forehead and the upturned tilt of her nose, lingering on the curve of her lips, smiling at the stubborn lift to her chin.

Did he really think he could turn back time to the way things used to be, with the taste of her on his lips and the memory of her curves pressed against him heating his blood and hardening his body? Did he really want to?

"So, what made you stop by, anyway?" she asked as she backed out of her driveway. "Don't tell me you have some kind of warning signal that goes off anytime I attempt a home improvement project on my own?"

He chuckled at that. "No, as far as I know, there's no such thing. Unfortunately." He waited for her to make a face at him before adding, "I thought, you know, with Bobby adopting Charlie that you'd be missing her."

"You came by to cheer me up?" she asked with a touch of surprise.

"Yeah, well—" He shrugged a shoulder, the faded gray Georgetown University T-shirt he wore suddenly feeling tight. *What are friends for?*

The words were on the tip of his tongue, but he didn't say them. Not when the flippant remark would only hurt Mollie, and not when he was starting to face the fact that his feelings for her were so much more than mere friendship.

Instead, he said, "I just wanted to make sure you were okay."

"I'm all right. I've got Arti and Chief."

And him, Zeke thought. She had him.

As Mollie headed toward town, driving well under the speed limit, she scanned the trees and brush lining either side of the road. Her caring and compassion never failed to amaze him. "I'll help you set some traps when we get back." He knew she wouldn't rest easy until the small stray was warm and safe with a home of its own.

Mollie shot him a grateful smile, one that had as much to do with how well he understood her as it did with his offer of help. "Thank you, Zeke."

"That wasn't so hard, was it?"

Slanting him a puzzled glance, she asked, "What?"

"Saying yes."

Her reddish-blond brows rose in challenge before she turned her attention back to the road. "You're the one who keeps saying no," she reminded him.

An hour later, Zeke and Mollie had loaded a flat-bed cart with the shutters, along with gallons of primer and paint Mollie picked out. He was surprised by how quickly and easily she'd selected the color. The last time his mother wanted to redecorate, the living room wall had looked like a Jackson Pollock painting for at least a month as she'd dabbed dozens of different colors over the surface, waiting for the right shade to "speak to her."

Evidently forest green spoke much more quickly to Mollie.

"We'll prime and paint the shutters first. Way easier

to do that on the ground than twenty feet in the air," he said as they maneuvered between towering rows of paint rollers, brushes and trays. "They'll look great once we get them installed."

Mollie mumbled something as she pushed the cart toward the registers at the front of the store. The rumble of squeaky wheels over the concrete floors must have affected his hearing, as all he caught was something about pigs. "What was that?"

Mollie sighed. "Something my mother said when I decided to paint the kitchen cabinets rather than tearing them out and updating the whole kitchen." Perfectly mimicking her mother's sugary-sweet Southern accent, she said, "'Honestly, Mollie, painting those old cabinets is like putting lipstick on a pig.'"

Reaching out, Zeke caught the crossbar, bringing Mollie and the cart to a sudden stop. "Hey." Unconcerned about the stream of customers heading up and down the aisle, he said, "I'm the one who told you to keep those cabinets in the first place, remember?"

Original to the house, the cabinets were made of real wood, built to last with tongue-and-groove joints and far more character than anything the home improvement store had to offer.

"I know, but you know my mother. She thought I should hire one of her decorators to redesign the whole space."

Georgia McFadden put his own mother to shame. He didn't know how many times over the years Mollie's mother had completely redecorated the stately home just a few houses down from where he'd grown up. The only thing that never changed was the collection of photographs and medals on the living room mantel above the ornate gray marble fireplace. A shrine that had been there long before Patrick passed away two years ago.

"Don't let her get to you."

"She doesn't...not really," Mollie insisted, but Zeke knew the words weren't entirely true. Though she had followed her own dreams, it bothered her that her parents didn't support her choices.

"You're amazing, Mollie. Don't ever forget that."

"I thought I was stubborn and headstrong and frustrating."

"Like I said. Amazing." Wrapping an arm around her waist, he pulled her close for a quick kiss in the middle of the paint aisle. One that felt so natural and right, he wondered why he hadn't been kissing Mollie for years.

Because for years, all you dreamed about was kissing Lilah, and look how that turned out when you finally got what you wanted. Zeke tried to ignore the annoying nudge from his conscience, but he couldn't deny how badly that relationship had ended for all involved. If he messed things up this time, he wouldn't have to worry about his parents losing a friend or about himself losing a fiancée.

He could lose Mollie. As a friend, as a lover, as the one person he counted on more than anyone in the world. All of which made him wonder if he knew what the hell he was doing.

"Hey." Reaching up, she ran her fingers along his jaw. "Everything okay?"

"Yeah, there's, um, a register opening up over there." After making it through the checkout without giving in to the urge to kiss Mollie again, Zeke wheeled the cart outside. "Why don't you bring the SUV up to the front of the store so we don't have to push this thing across the lot?"

As Mollie jogged across the asphalt, the late afternoon sun caught the golden highlights in her hair. Her cutoff shorts and Best Friends T-shirt showcased her toned arms and legs. More than one male had turned in appreciation on their way into the store, and Zeke had wanted to knock a couple of heads together for what they were thinking...which was exactly the same thing he was thinking.

Look out for her, would ya, Zeke? You know she likes to think she's tough, but she's all heart. And I don't want to see hers broken.

That was the last thing Zeke wanted, too. Especially if he was the man to do the breaking. His hands tightened on the cart handle at the thought. He'd already had one failed engagement and—

"Zeke? I thought that was you."

He turned, slightly incredulous, at the sound of the familiar voice. As if somehow summoned by his memories, Lilah Fairchild stood a few feet behind him. *Crap.* If his thoughts were going to suddenly start materializing out of nowhere, why the hell couldn't he have been thinking about pizza and beer?

"Lilah." Over two years had passed since he'd last seen her. With her long blond hair, ivory skin and dark blue eyes, she was as beautiful as ever. But compared to Mollie's warmth, her fire and passion, everything about his ex left him cold.

Dressed in a figure-hugging off-the-shoulder black knit blouse and leggings, she sashayed closer. "I suppose you already heard I was back."

Zeke nodded. *Bad news travels fast...* "I'm sure your parents are happy you're home." And maybe now they'd stop acting like he was the evil ex who'd run their little girl out of town.

"And you, Zeke?" Her bright red lips formed a slight pout. "Are you glad?"

The question was enough to make him want to laugh, but he wouldn't have said the reaction was from gladness. Instead, it was out of a sense of relief. If nothing else, seeing his former fiancée again gave an answer to a question that he hadn't realized until that moment had been lingering in his mind.

He was officially over Lilah Fairchild.

"Look, Lilah, I've got to go. Mollie's waiting for me—"

"Mollie?" Crossing her thin arms, she tossed her hair over her shoulder. "You're with Mollie? I thought she was seeing some other guy."

"How did—You know what? Never mind." He didn't care how Lilah knew about Mollie's date with Josh Sylvester, but he sure as hell didn't want to talk to Lilah about it. "Yes, I'm here with Mollie."

Lilah had always resented their friendship. She'd insinuated that there was something more than friendship between them, and like a fool, he'd been flattered by her jealousy. Now, though, he wondered if she hadn't picked up on a deeper awareness that he was only starting to acknowledge.

"Zeke, you should know—"

Lilah's words cut off as the automatic doors swooshed open and two guys wheeling out large sheets of plywood rumbled by with a couple of laughing teenaged boys jostling each other in their wake.

"I need to get going."

Lilah caught his arm before he could make his escape. The contrast of her hand—soft, slender, with perfectly French-manicured nails and a gold watch draped over her wrist—with Mollie's was as different as the emotion her touch elicited. When Mollie touched him, he wanted her to hold on and never let go. With Lilah, it was all he could do not to shake her off like something creepy-crawly had landed on his skin.

"We need to talk," she was saying, "about our engagement and how everything…ended."

Not long ago, Zeke would have given anything to have that talk. To finally understand what went wrong. Even now, a part of him still wanted to know. To learn what he'd done so he could move on, secure in the knowledge that he wouldn't make the same mistakes.

"You left, Lilah. End of story." Ignoring the locked wheel, Zeke gave the cart a strong shove and sent it rumbling across the asphalt. He didn't care if he looked like he was running away.

Lilah Fairchild was part of his past, and he was finally leaving her behind.

Before Mollie had a chance to back up in the crowded parking lot, Zeke wheeled over with all her purchases. "Hey." After shutting off the engine, she jumped out of the driver's seat and circled around to the back of the SUV. "I thought you were going to wait for me."

"Yeah, well…" Leaning against the cart's crossbar, his handsome face twisted into a wry grimace. "I had to make my escape while I could."

She laughed as she lowered the back hatch for him to load the shutters and other supplies inside. "Escape? Give me a break," she said as she reached for one of the gallons of paint. "You could spend days roaming around that store."

"Not while Lilah's inside."

The metal pail slipped from Mollie's fingers and landed with a thud. "Lilah?"

"Yeah, pretty much the last place I thought I'd see her, although I suppose I was bound to run into her sometime." The muscles in his arms flexed as he tossed the shutters into the back with a little more force than necessary. "Spring Forest's too small for us to avoid each other forever. Unfortunately."

Remembering what his ex had said about looking him up, Mollie muttered, "Especially if Lilah isn't looking to avoid you."

"Hey, I meant what I said at the barbecue. I'm over her. Seeing her today proved that like little else could."

"What—what did she have to say?"

Zeke shook his head as he swung the last of the paint into the back of the SUV. "She said we needed to get together and talk."

Mollie swallowed, her voice a mere croak as she asked, "About what?"

"About our breakup."

Oh, God… After all this time…why? Why now? Mollie jumped as Zeke slammed the back of the SUV closed, her nerves suddenly raw and exposed…vulnerable. "But that was years ago," she whispered.

"Yeah, that's pretty much what I told her. I mean, there was a time when not knowing why Lilah left ate me up inside but—what does it matter now?" he muttered as he thumped the side of his fist against the closed hatch.

It mattered. To a man like Zeke, of course it mattered. He wanted to know everything. He was the only person Mollie had ever met who read the directions through in their entirety before starting a project. He loved doing research when it came to fixing things around her house and going online to discover what it would take to train a service dog for Bobby.

He was not the type to leave anything unfinished, and his broken engagement was like a big ugly question mark hanging over their heads. For once, Mollie was the one with the answers.

Not answers, her conscience taunted her. *Secrets. Lies.*

Her stomach turned as the accusations echoed in her mind. For so many years, she had dreamed of something more than friendship with Zeke. But that relationship would be over before it started if she told Zeke the real reason his engagement with Lilah ended.

A few hours later, Zeke and Mollie had the shutters primed and painted and lying on sawhorses in Mollie's lush backyard to dry in the late afternoon sun. They'd have to hang them another day, but Zeke was happy with what they'd accomplished. Kneeling in the damp grass, he used the hose to clean the paint trays and rollers. Mollie laughed at him as the dogs made nuisances of themselves, excitedly dancing around, trying to chomp at the cool stream of water, and Zeke couldn't resist turning the hose on her.

Squealing, she dropped the brush she'd been cleaning and threw up her hands to block the spray. She shook the water from her hands before wiping the moisture from her face. Droplets darkened her hair to burgundy and dripped off the curled ends. He was half surprised the liquid didn't turn to steam as she glared at him, arms akimbo. "I can't believe you just did that!"

Her emerald T-shirt was too dark to turn transparent, but the wet material clung so faithfully to the curves of her breasts that it may as well have been invisible. Grinning, he hit her once more for good measure. "What about that?"

Mollie shrieked again, but this time dove for the nozzle, creating a mini fountain raining down over the both of them. The instant dousing did little to cool Zeke's blood as he caught her body to his. Mollie's gaze locked on his before dropping to his mouth, a whisper of invitation in her breathless gasp. Somewhere along the way, the hose fell to the ground, soaking their feet, but he barely noticed. Her lips were cool and refreshing beneath his, her tongue warm and wet, and a shudder racked the length of his spine.

Her fingers dug into his damp hair, and he forgot all about going slow. Forgot…everything but the sweet rush of desire and the arousing sounds Mollie made as he deepened the kiss.

She'd been quiet since they got back from the home improvement store. At first he hadn't noticed, too caught up in his own thoughts. Seeing Lilah had sent him into a bit of a funk. He'd avoided any serious relationships since his broken engagement, keeping his love life separate from Spring Forest and his encounters strictly casual.

Mollie was as big a part of Spring Forest as he was, and she deserved so much more than casual. Was that why she'd withdrawn as the afternoon went on? Was she having second thoughts about how far she wanted to go with a man who wasn't able to commit?

But now all he tasted was the eagerness in her kiss, the urgency of her touch as her hands raced from his shoulder blades down his spine to anchor at his hips. The soaked clothing between them was as inconsequential as the reasons he'd ever thought of taking things slow.

While they forgot about the running water and the hose, the dogs did not. With an almost violent jangle of dog tags, Chief gave a full body shake, flinging water and mud from the convenient bog he'd been rolling in all over Mollie and Zeke.

Mollie gasped as she was hit by the cold, wet splatter. The two of them sprang apart at the sudden shock. Her body trembling from the raw possessiveness of Zeke's kiss, she didn't know how she kept from collapsing into the oozing puddle right alongside her troublemaking dogs.

Lifting a hand, Zeke wiped a mud clot from beneath one eye. "Not exactly a cold shower—"

Shower... "Oh, good grief!" she gasped. "What time is it?"

"Um, I'm guessing half past mud bath." Zeke wasn't wearing a watch, and both of them had, wisely, left their cell phones inside. "Why?"

Mollie glanced down in horror. Her clothes had been nothing special to begin with, but now the green T-shirt and cutoff shorts were splattered and streaked with North Carolina soil. "I should already be getting ready."

Zeke frowned. "Ready for what?"

She pulled the wet T-shirt away from her chest, trying to ignore how clearly her breasts were revealed by the thin material. "Ready for my date with Josh."

Zeke's mud-spattered jaw dropped. "You are not serious."

"Well, I certainly can't go like this!" Throwing her arms out, she slogged across the saturated ground to turn the hose off at the spigot with a squeak of the pipes.

She couldn't believe she'd completely forgotten about her date! Between spotting the little stray terrier, Zeke showing up and the trip to the home improvement store, she'd had a lot going on. Not to mention it was hard to think of plans she'd made with another man when Zeke kept randomly showing up and kissing her!

But focusing on all of that only made it easier to ignore the real reason for her distraction.

Not knowing why Lilah left ate me up inside.

At the time of their breakup, Mollie had told him that Lilah must have realized she wasn't good enough for him. His ex didn't deserve him. Zeke deserved someone so much better... The truth, but not the whole truth, as to why Lilah had left.

And then, after Patrick died, Mollie and Zeke had grown even closer, and it was easy for her to pretend his engagement had never happened. That Zeke had gotten over Lilah and moved on. But she'd known it was a lie. The women he'd *moved on* to—nameless, faceless dates he never brought home to Spring Forest—proved he hadn't left the past behind or taken a step forward toward a lasting commitment.

Except he'd kissed her. She was about as far from his recent flings as a girl could get. And hadn't his suggestion that they take things slow intimated he was looking for a more serious relationship? So maybe he was over the breakup, after all. Or maybe she was just making excuses...

"Mollie. You can't—" He ran a hand through his hair only to pull back in disgust as his fingers came away covered in muck. With the chestnut strands sticking out in all directions and a predatory gleam in his eye as he cornered her against the shaded side of the house, he looked a little wild. So different from the cool, calm and collected Zeke she knew so well. "Cancel the date, Mollie."

Mollie swallowed, her throat bone-dry despite the rest of her being sopping wet. "Cancel at the last minute? That's totally rude."

"Not nearly as rude as me having to punch Josh Sylvester in the face when he shows up here tonight."

"You would never do that," she insisted, though something about the expression on Zeke's face seemed to say, *Try me*.

"Cancel the date, Mollie."

"Why?"

"Because I don't want you going out with Josh Sylvester."

Remembering what Matt Fielding had said about how the two of them hadn't been able to come up with a single guy to fix her up with, she demanded, "Have someone else in mind?"

"As a matter of fact," he vowed, the glint of gold in his hazel eyes burning bright as his gaze swept over her from head to toe and every aching, trembling space between, "I do."

Chapter Twelve

It's not a date.

Like the lyrics of an annoying pop song she couldn't get out of her head, Mollie kept repeating the words over and over again as she got ready that evening.

For what *wasn't* a date with Zeke Harper.

After canceling with Josh, she and Zeke had spent the next hour burning off the lingering sexual tension by chasing Arti and Chief around the huge yard. The dogs, who had gone crazy trying to catch water from the hose and who had rolled in canine bliss in the mud puddle, turned suddenly aquaphobic at the mention of a b-a-t-h.

By the time they'd finished, Mollie and Zeke were as wet—if not as clean—as the two dogs. After using some old towels to vigorously rub and dry the dogs into looking more like fluffy puppies than drowned rats,

Mollie had innocently offered to throw Zeke's clothes into the washer.

He'd given her a long look, and just like that, the desire she thought they'd doused out in the backyard flickered to life once more. Nerves had shot off in her belly like skyrockets. Though Zeke hadn't said so, Mollie had the feeling that if either one of them took their clothes off, it wouldn't be for anything as mundane as doing the laundry.

Instead, he'd borrowed one of her towels to cover the seat of his car so he could drive home, and then he'd kissed her. The quick yet heated embrace had left her breathless and panting for more, but Zeke had only given her a slightly smug grin before asking, "Come to my place tonight? Around seven?"

Mollie was pretty sure she'd nodded as she watched him walk away, his damp white T-shirt clinging to wide shoulders and the muscles of his back. Any capability of speech or thought had been beyond her at that moment.

But in the hours since, she'd had more than enough time to question what the invitation really meant.

For all she knew, he just wanted to celebrate their combined triumph after everything had gone so well with Bobby and Charlie. Nothing more. Even so, as Mollie stared into the mirror above the bathroom sink at the crazy curls she'd pulled back into a ponytail, at the freckles shining out from a makeup-free face, at the lips highlighted only by a slight shine from the balm she favored, she was tempted to reach for the small beauty bag Amanda had left behind for her.

It's not a date.

And even if it was, she was going to take her own advice and be herself.

Flicking off the light, she went into the kitchen to

check on the dogs. Kneeling down, she rubbed Arti's silky ears before giving Chief a scratch on the soft fur beneath his chin. The dog tipped his head back, his eyes closing in sheer canine bliss. "Be good puppies, okay? I'll be home soon."

She gave each dog a treat before she grabbed her purse and headed out.

Though Zeke's invitation might not have been a date, Mollie's mother had always taught her not to arrive anywhere empty-handed, and even friends could share a celebratory bottle of wine. With that in mind, she stopped by the grocery store.

She didn't know much about wine, and row after row of bottles gleaming beneath the fluorescent lights was somewhat overwhelming. But when she spotted one with the outline of a dog jumping through a hoop on the label, she quickly made her choice.

With the bottle tucked under her arm, she headed for the express checkout. The woman in line in front of her glanced back with a smile that turned into a double take. "Mollie McFadden?"

"Um, yes…" Racking her brain trying to figure out if she knew the pretty, dark-haired woman, Mollie drew a blank. Definitely not one of her pet parents or anyone she could recall running into at Furever Paws.

When the other woman's eyes filled with tears, curiosity turned to a bit of panic. "Oh, my goodness!" the woman exclaimed. *"Thank you."*

Mollie didn't have a chance to respond before the woman wrapped her in a somewhat awkward hug with the wine bottle caught between them. "Um, you're welcome?"

"I'm so sorry." The woman pulled back with a

slightly embarrassed laugh. "You don't even know who I am, do you? My name's Amy Doyle."

"Bobby's wife."

Amy nodded as she wiped at the tears in her eyes. "Yes, and I assure you I don't typically go around hugging perfect strangers. I should have reached out to you already to tell you how amazing you are."

More than a little uncomfortable with the other woman's praise, along with the attention they were garnering from the nearby shoppers, Mollie shook her head. "I should be thanking you. Everyone at Furever Paws is always so grateful when families look to adopt a pet."

Amy gave a soft laugh. "Charlie isn't just a pet. Not to us. I've seen those bumper stickers before. You know the ones that say My Dog Rescued Me? But I never truly understood until I saw Bobby with Charlie."

"So, everything is going well?" Mollie knew both Zeke and Matt had been checking in with the vet since he took Charlie home. She planned to continue to work with Charlie and to include Bobby in the dog's training, but she'd wanted to give them a chance to bond first. She wanted the Lab to see Bobby—and not her—as the human Charlie needed to follow.

"It's been amazing. I haven't seen Bobby so happy since…" The woman's voice trailed off, leaving behind the unspoken horrors no one but the veterans who'd experienced them could truly understand.

"And it's all thanks to you," Amy finished.

Mollie shook her head. "You're giving me far too much credit. Matt and Zeke were the ones with the idea of finding a dog for Bobby. And Charlie, I mean, she's the perfect dog. I really didn't have to do much of anything."

"You have to see them together." Amy's eyes lit. "In fact, we're having a get-together this weekend. I wanted to throw a party a long time ago, but Bobby wasn't up for the idea of hanging out in a big crowd. Now, though, he can't wait to show off how smart Charlie is. You and Zeke have to come!"

Mollie wasn't sure what to think of the other woman linking her name with Zeke's, but Mollie reassured Amy that she would talk to him about the party. "I hope to see the two of you there. And have fun on your date tonight," Amy said with the glance at the wine before she wheeled her cart toward the exit.

It's not a date...and we're not a couple.

Despite the reminder, Mollie couldn't quell the excitement and anticipation building inside her as she thanked the cashier and headed for the exit. Maybe she was wrong. Maybe tonight would change things between them—

Mollie stopped short as she caught sight of Lilah Fairchild standing in front of the automatic doors. "Little Miss Mollie," she said, her bright red lips curled into a sardonic grin. "Everyone thinks you're so perfect."

Mollie clutched the bottle of wine to her chest as her jaw dropped. "Me?" she asked incredulously. "*No one* thinks—"

"But that would change, wouldn't it," the other woman continued, "if they knew the truth." She stepped closer, towering over Mollie with her height and heels. "If Zeke knew how you blackmailed me into breaking up with him."

Mollie's gut twisted at the thought. "It wasn't blackmail," she whispered.

"'Tell him the truth or I will,'" Lilah quoted word for word from that night just over two years ago.

"But you *didn't* tell him," Mollie argued.

"And neither did you," Lilah said, her beautiful features twisted into a smug expression.

"What would have been the point?" Mollie asked. "The two of you had already broken up, and you'd moved a continent away. Why would I hurt Zeke by telling him then?"

What would have been the point of telling Zeke the woman he loved, the woman he'd been engaged to, had cheated on him? Even after all this time, Mollie could still remember the icy shock and the red-hot fury at discovering how Lilah, who had *everything* Mollie had ever wanted, could be unfaithful.

Lilah scoffed. "Oh, please! You weren't protecting Zeke. You were protecting yourself…and your brother."

Mollie's stomach churned at the accusation.

"That's not true," she whispered hollowly. "Patrick was…"

For a brief second, Mollie saw some emotion flash in the other woman's gaze. But it was gone as quickly as it had come, and when Lilah leaned forward, her dark eyes were flat and cold. "All this time, you kept silent. And you finally have Zeke Harper exactly where you've always wanted him. So now it's my turn. Tell him the truth…or I will."

Tell him or I will…

Mollie had never had her own words come back to hit her with such a vengeance. And while she wasn't sure she would have ever acted on her own threat, she had no doubt Lilah would see her vow through to the bitter end. And while Lilah should have been the one to shoulder the blame for her actions back then, to carry the weight of her own betrayal, Mollie couldn't let Zeke hear about the affair—or about Mollie's role in keeping it hidden—from his ex.

As bad as the truth was, Lilah would undoubtedly make the telling of it that much worse. Not to mention what she might say about Patrick. Her brother might have looked out for her while he was alive, but now that he was gone, Mollie was the one to honor his memory as best she could.

Which meant, like it or not, Lilah was right. She needed to tell Zeke the truth.

Her earlier excitement and anticipation deflated as quickly as a hapless beach ball left in Arti's clutches. An evening intended for celebration was going to turn out very differently than either of them planned.

The familiar drive to Zeke's apartment went by all too fast, and before she knew it, she was knocking on his door. He answered almost instantly, as if he'd been waiting on the other side. His huge grin hit Mollie hard, knowing she'd soon be wiping the happy expression from his face.

"Hey, Mollie."

Her greeting stalled in her throat when he leaned forward to kiss her cheek. An innocent enough brush of his lips against her skin, and yet her reaction was anything but innocent. Desire pooled inside her belly at his clean, masculine scent.

Not knowing what else to do, she shoved the bottle at his chest. "I brought wine."

"Just what we need to celebrate." Only she didn't need alcohol. She didn't need anything more than Zeke looking at her as he was in that moment to make her head spin. "Come on in."

With the wine in one hand, he took her arm as if he was escorting her on a red carpet walkway rather than across the warm hardwood of his living room. "Zeke, there's something I have to tell you," she began.

"Me first," he interrupted with another smile. "Or show you, at least."

He didn't say anything more as they passed through the kitchen. He took her purse and set it and the bottle of wine on the black granite island before he led the way toward the dining room. An oddly colorful glow spilled out from the doorway, but nothing could have prepared her for the sight that greeted her as she stepped inside. Mollie stared, speechless, at the room in front of her. Zeke's functional and somewhat staid dining room, with its light oak floors and farmhouse-style table and chairs, had been transformed into—into…Mollie didn't know what.

"What is all this?" she asked as she took in the lighted three-foot Christmas tree centerpiece, complete with two dozen or so red-and-green glass bulbs; the heart-shaped balloons bobbing on strings tied to the backs of the chairs; the bright green shamrocks twirling from streamers attached to the ceiling; the Easter eggs scattered across the table along with a stuffed bunny smiling out from a woven pastel basket; and the red, white and blue sparklers stuck in a carved jack-o'-lantern that shared space with a cartoon cutout turkey. "Did a Party City explode in your house?"

Zeke grinned at her shocked expression. "Something like that." His smile faded, though, as he plucked a red rose out of a crystal vase on the table and trailed the tender bud over her cheek and across her lips. The heat in his eyes and the petal-soft touch had her legs trembling.

"Zeke…"

"This is Christmas, Mollie. It's New Year's and Valentine's Day. It's St. Patrick's Day and Easter and the

Fourth of July. It's every holiday you've missed since your brother died."

The conviction in his deep voice grabbed hold of the longing inside of her, of the long-buried hopes and dreams and wishes, and made her believe. In Christmas miracles, in New Year's resolutions, in Valentine's hearts and flowers, in the luck of the Irish…

Her lips parted, but no sound escaped. What could she possibly say? No one, not her brother, not her parents, not her friends, had ever done something so sweet, so amazing for her. Tears pricked the back of her eyes. "I can't believe you did all this."

He waved his hand at the holiday bonanza behind him. "You deserve it, Mollie."

And just like that, the guilt she'd been battling since Lilah's return hit full force. Setting the rose he'd handed her aside, she protested, "I'm not—"

"You are, Mollie. You're the most amazing woman I've ever known. You're kind and caring and brave and passionate." His voice deepened on the final word, setting off some of those Fourth of July sparklers in her belly. "You deserve to celebrate every holiday. Hell, you deserve to celebrate every day."

She shook her head, tears blurring her vision and clogging her throat. She didn't need a year's worth of holidays. She just needed one night. One night to spend with Zeke before she told him the secret she'd kept from him for far too long. "Did you hear that?" she whispered around the ache of longing in her throat.

Zeke frowned. "Hear what?" he asked, his eyebrows drawing together in question.

"I think the countdown's starting."

"The countdown?"

"To midnight."

"Ah," he said, catching on, "because it's twelve o'clock somewhere."

Mollie shook her head. "Not yet. We still have time. Ten…nine…eight…" With each second she counted down, the heat in Zeke's eyes ratcheted up. "Seven… six…"

She never made it to five as Zeke plunged his fingers into her hair, holding her still for his kiss when Mollie couldn't have moved—wouldn't have moved—to save her life.

Eager for the feel of him, she ran her hands up and down his back. The thin black polo he wore wasn't much of a barrier. The heat of his body burned through the material, and the easy slide of the shirt hinted at the smooth skin beneath. Skin that she wanted to feel sliding against her own.

Desire flowed through her veins, leaving her weak, breathless and astounded by how quickly the rush came over her. She'd never felt like this before, so out of control, so head over heels, so ready to take this next step.

Her head spun as if she'd consumed a bottle of champagne and goose bumps rose over her skin. "Zeke…"

His name escaped her in a gasp as he lifted his head, breaking the kiss for a split second, for an eternity. His green-gold eyes burned into hers. "Are you sure, Mollie?"

Sure she loved him? Sure she wanted this? Sure her world was about to change and nothing would ever be the same again? Mollie gave the only answer she could. "Yes."

Taking her at her whispered word, Zeke kissed her again. So caught up in the teasing, tantalizing kiss, she barely noticed when he swept her off her feet and into his arms. She clung to his shoulders as he carried her

down the hall. Mollie had been to his apartment numer-
ous times over the years, but she'd never set foot inside
his bedroom. Another time, she might have taken more
note of the masculine navy-and-tan color scheme, but
in that moment, all she saw, felt, tasted was Zeke. The
molten flecks of gold in his hazel eyes, the weight of
his body as he covered hers on the wide expanse of his
bed, the salt and seduction of his kiss.

Mollie was only vaguely aware of pulling her shirt
over her head and tugging Zeke's from his broad shoulders. As his gaze dropped to her breasts, she had a
moment to wish she'd worn some of the sexy lingerie
she'd bought at the shop in Raleigh. But if the heat in
his gaze was anything to go by, he didn't care that her
bra was white cotton rather than vivid colored silk.
In the split second it took him to brush the utilitarian
cups from her breasts, she figured any money she spent
would have been somewhat wasted anyway since his
only interest in the bra seemed to be in discarding it.
Perhaps next time…if there was a next time.

Pushing that worry from her thoughts, Mollie turned
her focus to this time. This first time. With Zeke. With
any man.

Her eager hands charted a course over his broad
shoulders and leanly defined arms. It had always
amazed her a little, how he could be so smart and still
so sexy. His muscles jerked beneath his smooth skin
at her touch, the slight reactions fascinating her even
more.

"Mollie…"

He groaned her name as he broke off the heated
kiss. Reading the struggle written in his tense jaw, she
found herself cursing the *smart* part. Didn't he realize
she was so much more interested in exploring the *sexy*

at the moment? If he couldn't turn off that big brain of his, she had the feeling he would stop. Stop kissing her, stop touching her, stop taking his clothes off, and that was the last thing she wanted.

Mollie had never considered herself particularly bold or sexy, but then again, she'd never been in Zeke's bed before. Taking his face in her hands, she murmured, "Don't stop. Don't think. Just feel."

And with more guts than it took to face down a one hundred and thirty-pound rottweiler, she took one of his hands and brought it to her naked breast. His fingers curved around her flesh, and her nipple instantly tightened in his palm. "Mollie," he gasped, "you're driving me crazy here."

"That is the idea," she whispered, arching into his touch. She'd waited so long, she didn't care if it was crazy, didn't care that it would change everything. In that moment, all she cared about was Zeke. Everything he was willing to give, and all she feared he never would. Mollie might have been innocent, but she wasn't naive. She knew making love didn't equal falling in love. But she still had hope that Zeke might one day see her as someone he could care for and not just someone to take care of.

She wasn't sure how the rest of their clothes were tossed aside. All she knew was that Zeke was touching her, caressing, bringing her to a point of pleasure she'd never imagined. His hot palm laid claim to the bare skin of her belly before moving lower. The air evaporated from her lungs as waves of heat washed over her and she cried out his name.

Still trembling from the aftershocks that had turned her inside out, leaving her heart and soul completely exposed, Mollie panicked when Zeke pulled away. Surely he wasn't leaving—but he was only gone an instant, the time it took for him to grab protection, and then he was back, covering her body with his. Erasing that split second of vulnerability and doubt with the heat and hunger of his kiss.

Eager and desperate for him, Mollie ran her hands from his shoulders down his spine as he kissed her neck, her breasts, her belly before moving back up her body. Leaving her breathless and longing for more. Zeke wanted her, and Mollie told herself it was enough even as she tensed in that final moment as his body sank between her thighs. She gasped slightly at the moment of penetration, but it was Zeke who froze, his eyes wide with shock as he discovered one of the secrets she'd been keeping. Her hands clutched at the smooth muscles of his back. "Don't stop, Zeke," she whispered. "Please."

"Stop?" he groaned. "We're just getting started."

And as he gazed down at her, the mix of tenderness and passion in his sharp features so clear, so perfect as he moved within her, stoking her desire until the flames consumed her, Mollie could almost—almost—believe it was love.

Chapter Thirteen

Mollie wasn't sure exactly what to expect the next morning, but it wasn't waking up in Zeke's bed alone. Early morning sunlight sliced through a part in the curtains, highlighting the empty space beside her. He'd pulled up the sheets and straightened the blankets, and if she hadn't been naked and her body slightly tender in places it had never been tender before, she might have thought she'd dreamed the entire night.

A night that had been so amazing, so incredible. She'd done more than completely give Zeke her body, she'd irrevocably handed him her heart. And Zeke... He'd been so tender, so passionate. She'd looked into his eyes as he claimed her that first time, so sure she saw something more than desire reflected there and yet... she'd been wrong before, hadn't she?

Holding the sheet to her breasts, she sat up and glanced around the room. Her hands clenched in the soft navy cotton as she spotted her clothes neatly folded into a perfectly square pile on the top of Zeke's dresser. So different from how they'd been scattered across the room the night before, almost as if he was trying to tidy away what had happened.

She slid out of the bed on shaky legs, the oak floors cold against her feet. Maybe she was overreacting. Maybe she was making too big a deal out of waking alone in Zeke's bed.

Somehow she didn't think so.

After prolonging what was starting to feel like an inevitable heartbreak by wasting time in the bathroom, her hands trembled a bit as she dressed, her fingers fumbling with the clasp of her plain white bra, with the zipper and button on her shorts. She retraced her steps down the hallway, trying to block the memory of Zeke carrying her the night before. She didn't dare look into the dining room, focusing instead on the kitchen where her foolishly optimistic heart hoped she might find him happily preparing for breakfast in bed.

The sunny room was empty, as well, with no hint of coffee percolating in the state-of-the-art brewer or bacon sizzling on the glass-top stove. The sudden familiar ringtone of her cell seemed startlingly loud in the silent space. Spotting her purse on the large granite island where Zeke had placed it the night before, she pulled out her phone.

She didn't recognize the number flashing across the screen, but she answered anyway. "Is this Mollie McFadden?" a female voice asked over the din of barking dogs in the background.

Assuming the call was work related, Mollie did her best to pull herself together. She rubbed at her aching forehead as if she could somehow wipe away the doubts circling within. "This is Mollie."

"This is Selena Martinez at the county shelter in Asheville. I believe we have one of your dogs here."

Mollie's heart took a ten-story drop. "No, that's not possible."

"Your dogs are all with you?"

"Well, no, but—" She'd fed them and locked them inside the house before she'd left for Zeke's the evening before. She lived far enough outside of town that she didn't risk leaving them outside at night when she wasn't home.

Arti could be a bit of an escape artist given the opportunity, but not even the super-smart hound had figured out how to unlock doors. "I don't know how they could have gotten out of the house. Are you sure it's one of my dogs?"

"Her tags registered to you." Some of the woman's professionalism slipped a bit as she said, "She's such a sweet Lab."

A sweet Lab...

"Charlie?" Any relief she might have felt that Arti and Chief were safe immediately disappeared into a far greater worry over Charlie...and Bobby. Her fingers tightened around the phone as she explained, "I was Charlie's foster for the past few weeks." Since they never knew how long it would take before a dog was adopted, Furever Paws's policy was to register the dogs with their fosters. "She was recently adopted."

Images of that first meeting between Bobby and Charlie flashed through Mollie's mind. She'd seen the immediate bond between Bobby and the sensitive dog. She couldn't imagine the vet letting her out of his sight. With the comings and goings of a busy family, a door might have been left open and most dogs would quickly take the opportunity to run free. Most dogs. But Charlie...

"Do you know where she was found?"

When the woman named an isolated back road almost two hours outside of town, Mollie clutched her free arm over her stomach. No way could the dog wander that far. Not unless she'd been gone for hours and if that was the case, then why—

"Mollie!"

She heard the back door open as Zeke called out her name. Quickly reassuring the woman from the county shelter that she would pick up Charlie right away, Mollie pocketed the phone.

She didn't have a chance to prepare herself before Zeke stepped into the kitchen. He wore a faded gray T-shirt and black gym shorts, and Mollie wished she could believe that he'd simply gone out for a run and had planned to be back before she awoke. But the slightly haggard expression and shadows beneath his eyes told a different story.

Time seemed to stretch out between them as their gazes met, filled with everything Mollie wanted to say and everything she feared Zeke didn't want to hear. Finally, he lifted the cell phone in his hand. "I just got a call from Amy. When she woke up this morning, Bobby was gone. She expected him back hours ago, and she's getting worried."

Mollie swallowed, wishing she could say something to ease his concern. Instead, she filled him in on the call from the shelter. "I'm going to go get Charlie and bring her home."

She doubted bringing the dog back would offer Amy

or the kids much comfort while Bobby was still missing, but it was the one thing she could do.

"I'll go with you."

Mollie hesitated as she reached into her purse for her keys. The last thing she wanted was an awkward, tension-filled ride to the shelter, but in that moment, they had bigger concerns than her bruised feelings. With a short nod, she led the way out of the kitchen. Her steps faltered as she passed by the dining room with its explosion of decorations. The heart-shaped balloons still held more than enough helium to keep them floating along, but for Mollie, it was as if all the air had gotten sucked right out of her lungs, leaving her light-headed and dizzy.

Zeke nearly bumped into her from behind, catching her by the shoulders when she stopped short. She felt his chest expand, brushing up against her shoulder blades. "Mollie…"

The husky murmur was far too reminiscent of the way he'd whispered in her ear, but where passion had filled his voice the night before, in the bright light of the morning, Mollie heard only the deep, discordant undertone of regret. Unable to bear it if he told her the night she'd been dreaming of, the night she'd been waiting for, was nothing more than a mistake, she quickly pulled away.

"Does Amy have any idea where Bobby might have gone?"

"No, she said he didn't leave any kind of note or anything… He's been walking with Charlie early in the morning, but today his truck's gone."

And Charlie was in a shelter in the next county.

A few minutes later, as Mollie headed toward the shelter in Asheville, Zeke called Matt. She could tell by the half of the conversation she could hear that Amy had already called the other man. "Where?"

At Mollie's quick glance, Zeke shook his head. "The police found Bobby's truck."

Waiting for him to finish the call, Mollie asked, "The police? Bobby's only been gone a few hours…"

"Too soon for any kind of missing persons report," Zeke agreed, "but Matt has some friends on the force and asked them to keep an eye out. A ranger was investigating a report of illegal camping and found Bobby's truck near the turnout at Sutter's Point."

Mollie's hands tightened on the wheel. She was familiar with the nature preserve. Nearly every year hikers got lost in the vast forest. Her stomach twisted at the thought that Bobby might have gone there not wanting to be found.

Seeming to have the same thought, Zeke rubbed both hands over his face before he muttered beneath his breath. "That place is huge."

"Yes, but at least now we know where to look."

"You're talking about hundreds of acres. If Bobby's in some kind of trouble, how could we possibly find him?"

"You and I can't." Forcing a confidence she wasn't feeling into her voice, Mollie insisted, "But I know who can."

Go find…

Two hours after Mollie had given that command, they were still trailing behind Arti as the hound's nose swept over every rock and leaf and twig along the path cutting through the dense forest.

What little faith Zeke had in the dog finding the missing man dwindled with each passing second.

Though the trees blocked the worst of the sun, the midmorning heat and humidity had sweat gathering at his temples and running down his face. Mollie's ponytail had lost its typical bounce and curl, hanging limply against the side of her neck.

A slight red mark abraded the tender flesh. A mark he himself had left there only hours earlier as they'd made love.

He'd been her first.

Zeke hadn't expected that or the sudden attack of conscience that had finally driven him from his own bed. He'd known how shy Mollie could be and that she didn't date much, but he'd never guessed she was a virgin. But the shock of that hadn't been enough to make him stop. Not that first time or later in the night when they'd made love again.

He didn't know what time it was when he eased away from the warmth of Mollie's body. He'd intended to do no more than get some water from the kitchen, but somehow he'd ended up on his back patio, sitting on the steps and staring at the sun creeping over the horizon.

The location hadn't escaped his attention or done anything to ease his guilt. He'd sat in that same spot with Patrick on his last visit home. He had tried on that final day to get his friend to open up about the shadows in his eyes, the distance he felt even when Patrick was sitting right beside him.

Don't worry about me, man.

You're my best friend, Patrick. I want you to take care of yourself over there.

Looking out for myself... Patrick had given a short laugh. *That is the one thing I'm good at.*

Patrick—

You want to do something for me? Take care of Mollie...

If Patrick knew what Zeke had done—

He shoved the thought from his mind as he pushed forward. He couldn't think about that now. Adding another layer of guilt to the load he carried would likely crush him.

The two of them had barely talked since meeting Matt at the garage to pick up one of Bobby's T-shirts. Matt had wanted to join them on the search, but Zeke had encouraged the other man to go over to the Doyles' house. Mollie had called the Whitaker sisters, as well, who had immediately offered to pick up Charlie from the shelter and take her back home to be with Amy as she waited for news.

None of them wanted to voice their fears about how bad the news might be.

Mollie stumbled slightly as Arti jerked on the leash, doubling back to go over the same small patch of ground she'd already spent five minutes sniffing. Frustrated, he rubbed the back of his hand across his sweating forehead. He understood the need to do something, but this?

Sure, he'd seen what the dog could do, but finding Mollie—Arti's human and the person the dog was most attached to—right outside her own backyard was one thing.

Finding a total stranger in vast acres of wilderness... That was something else.

He opened his mouth, ready to suggest they head back, when Mollie knelt down beside her dog. She held the T-shirt out again. "Go find, Arti. You can do it, baby girl. I know you can."

Her voice shook as she wrapped an arm around her

dog's neck and Arti turned her head to give her mistress's face a quick lick, almost as if offering comfort.

Dammit, if anyone should be comforting Mollie...

But when he bent down to help her to her feet, Mollie instantly pulled away. She glared at him even as she wiped the tears Arti had missed from her freckled cheeks. "Don't," she warned. "We're not going back. We're not giving up."

"We're not giving up, but Mollie, we don't even know if we're on the right track."

"*Arti* knows!" she insisted. "And I—" Her voice cracked on the word, and for a split second her face started to crumple. "I saw Amy yesterday. She gave me a hug to thank me for helping Bobby and told me how amazing I was. I can't give up, Zeke, I just can't!"

"Okay, Mollie, we'll keep going." Swinging the pack off his back, he unzipped it and handed her a bottle of water. He didn't know if they would find Bobby or not, but he wanted to be prepared either way. "You won't be doing Bobby any good if you pass out out here."

She looked ready to argue but nodded instead. She gulped down half the bottle and then pulled out a collapsible vinyl bowl from her back pocket for Arti and poured out the rest of the water for her dog.

For the next minute, the only sound was Arti eagerly lapping up the lukewarm liquid. Once the dog finished, Mollie folded up the bowl. She let the dog sniff the T-shirt again before determinedly commanding the dog to find.

"Did Amy say anything when you talked to her on the phone?" she asked, her words rising and falling as they stepped up and over knee-high boulders and thick bushes. "Any explanation for what might have set Bobby

off? She was so happy when I saw her at the store, and
I thought—"

"What?"

"I really thought Charlie had done it, you know?" An
ache of tears filled her voice. "That she was enough to
help Bobby adjust to being back home."

Zeke caught her by the arm and forced her to look
at him. "Listen to me! This is not your fault. You did
an amazing job training Charlie. I wanted to think it
would be enough, too, and I'm the one trained to help
people. I couldn't help Bobby..."

The guilt that had been festering for so long started
spilling out. He'd tried to bury the emotion, but now it
was like a landslide, and everything he'd piled on only
added to the relentless, destructive deluge hurtling
straight toward him. "Just like I couldn't help Patrick."

Mollie stilled at his touch, freezing at the shock of
his words, and Zeke could feel the chill right down to
his soul. "What do you mean you couldn't help Patrick?"

"His last visit home I knew something was bothering him, but I couldn't get him to talk to me." He'd
been too busy with his own problems to see how badly
his friend, his *best* friend, needed help. He'd let Patrick
go back to his unit, to the danger-filled job of being a
soldier, without getting him to face whatever had been
troubling him. "If I had—"

"Zeke, no. You can't blame yourself!"

A pleading note had entered Mollie's voice, and her
eyes, so wide and wounded in her pale face, were begging him to deny the truth he'd known since Patrick's
death. A truth he couldn't hide from her anymore even
though she would never forgive him.

He didn't deserve Mollie's forgiveness. He didn't deserve Mollie.

"I let him go back even though I knew something big—something bad—was weighing on his mind. I let him go, Mollie, and I got him killed."

Chapter Fourteen

Oh, God...

"Zeke... You can't think that!" Shock and guilt crashed through Mollie at the pain etched across his ravaged features. "You can't!"

His shoulders dropped and his head fell back as he stared unseeing at the towering trees overhead. A shudder racked his tall frame as he sucked in a shaky breath, and Mollie's heart ached at the sound. She hadn't seen him so distraught, so vulnerable since—

Since Patrick's death.

For two years, he'd been carrying around the grief and guilt that looked ready to crush him now. All because of the secret she'd kept.

You weren't protecting Zeke. You were protecting yourself...

Lilah's accusation seemed to echo throughout the nature preserve until Mollie wanted to throw her hands over her ears to block out the sound. But the truth couldn't be silenced.

Mollie had been protecting herself. Protecting the friendship that had meant so much to her for over a decade. *Patrick, Zeke and Mollie*. It had always been the three of them, and Lilah's presence had already driven a wedge between them before Patrick's last trip home. Mollie had been so afraid to do anything that might change the small spot she occupied in his life.

She was still afraid. Wasn't that why she'd settled for friendship for so many years rather than telling Zeke how she truly felt? Willing to accept what little she could get instead of taking a risk and reaching for it all? Always just tagging along...

And now, in trying to protect herself, she'd hurt Zeke in ways she couldn't imagine.

"What happened to Patrick was not your fault. None of it was your fault!"

Shaking his head, he scraped a rough hand through his damp hair. "I know what I saw in Patrick on that last visit home. He was...troubled, Mollie. Maybe you didn't see it. Patrick never wanted to let you or your parents see how haunted he was by the things he'd seen... the things he'd done..."

It was true that Mollie didn't know much about Patrick's life as a soldier. He'd always wanted to protect her just like she had wanted to protect him...and to protect Zeke. All of them keeping secrets with the best of intentions and the worst of results.

"I wanted to help him. I tried but—I failed. If whatever was bothering him made him careless, made him take chances he shouldn't have been taking—"

Mollie planted her palm straight in Zeke's chest. "Patrick was your best friend, but he was also my brother! I know he could be reckless at times, and I have no doubt he risked his life—probably on a daily basis—because that was what the army asked of him. But he had every intention of coming back home. Who do you think gave me the idea of training Arti for scent work?"

She waved a hand at the hound, straining at the end of the leash. "Patrick was so impressed with the K-9 units overseas. It was something he wanted to get involved in when he got out of the service. We were going to expand the business and work together. That was his plan for the future, and we talked about it all of the time, even during that last visit home. Right up to the days before he died."

Zeke was silent for a moment, as if letting her words sink in. "Patrick never told me any of that."

"He didn't tell you everything," Mollie said, hollowly. Including the secret she'd been keeping. *Tell him the truth...*

"Zeke, that last time Patrick came home—"

Mollie didn't have a chance to say more as the wind shifted and Arti let out a sudden, startling howl. Mollie stumbled as the dog surged forward, nearly pulling the leash from her grasp and jerking her right off her feet. She had little choice but to follow, her tennis shoes pounding against the rocky pathway at a full run as she tried to keep up with the hound.

Zeke's longer legs kept stride as he jogged beside her. "Do you think—"

"I don't know," she said, even as she whispered a prayer that Arti had found the missing man and that Bobby was all right. His family was so worried, and Zeke—

If Bobby didn't make it, Zeke would never forgive himself...like he had never forgiven himself for Patrick.

And that was all her fault.

Up ahead, the pathway curved to the left, but instead of making the turn, Arti lunged into the bushes on the right and disappeared.

"Mollie…"

She heard the doubt in Zeke's voice, but she wasn't giving up. Not on Arti and not on Bobby. He had to be okay. He just had to be. "I think she's scented on something, Zeke. I really do."

She ducked beneath the branches of an oak tree, wincing as low-growing bushes scraped at her skin. The leash was pulled as taut as a tightrope as Mollie tried to follow the route her dog had taken. Arti's howls increased, and the clamoring sound had Mollie ignoring the slight sting to dive deeper into the underbrush. She stumbled slightly on the downward slope but kept pushing forward. She heard Zeke thrashing through the brush behind her, having a harder time maneuvering his larger frame through the dense growth.

"Mollie!" Frustration filled his voice. "Wait for me."

But she didn't dare slow down. Not when it would mean giving up hope that Arti had found Bobby. Not when stopping would mean she had no choice but to tell Zeke the truth.

She almost fell again as Arti changed direction, cutting back toward the right and leaping over a fallen log. She stumbled after the dog, rough wood scraping her palms as she scrambled over a tree at the bottom of a ravine.

Her shoulders dropped as Arti sat back on her haunches, and she feared the dog had lost the scent, but then Arti tipped her long-eared head back and howled.

Chills ran down Mollie's spine. As a hound dog, Arti was rarely silent. She barked at squirrels, at birds, at mailmen. She barked when it was time to eat and whenever Mollie hinted at the word *walk*. But as noisy as the dog was, Mollie recognized all of those barks. This howl that meant she'd locked in on the scent.

At first, Mollie didn't see anything other than the shades of green and brown underbrush at the bottom of the ravine, but then a hint of black caught her eye. Black rubber soles. Black leather boots. The camouflage fatigues blended in with the forest floor, but then Mollie made out the shape of a fallen man.

"Zeke!" She grabbed his arm as he skidded to a stop beside her in a small landslide of loose dirt, rocks and leaves. "There!" Mollie crossed her arms over her stomach, sick with worry as Zeke knelt by Bobby's side. "Is he…" She couldn't get the words out as she prayed they weren't too late.

"He's breathing. His pulse is steady." She watched as Zeke checked the unconscious man's vitals. "He's got a contusion on his forehead. Probably from the fall."

Even as Zeke spoke, Bobby let out a low groan, the sound the best thing Mollie had heard since Arti's exuberant howl. Kneeling down by her dog, Mollie ran her hands over her beloved hound's silky ears. "Good girl, Arti. Such a good girl," she praised as she pulled out the small bag of dried liver treats the dog lived for—a reward for a job well done.

"Take it easy," Zeke was telling Bobby as the other man tried to sit up. "You took a pretty big fall. We need to make sure you don't have any broken bones before you try to move. Does anything hurt?"

As Zeke slowly helped Bobby into a sitting position, Mollie could see how pale he was, his ashen skin a stark contrast to the purplish bruise and swelling above his eye. "My head's killing me…and my ankle's throbbing something fierce."

Zeke pushed up the man's pants leg to reveal the swelling starting right above the top of his boot. "You probably have a concussion and either a serious sprain or even a break in that ankle. Do you remember what happened?"

"I was out with Charlie and—Charlie!" Despite the knot on his forehead and twisted ankle, Bobby immediately tried to push to his feet. "I have to find her!"

Zeke clamped a hand on Bobby's shoulder. "She's okay. She's already been found and is safe in a shelter in Asheville."

"I called the Whitakers on the way over here," Mollie told him. "They offered to pick Charlie up and to take her back to your house where she belongs."

"That's—" Bobby had to clear his throat before finishing. "That's good. If anything happened to her—"

"She's fine," Zeke reassured him, "and you were going to tell us how you fell."

Bobby winced as he touched his forehead. "I haven't been here in years, but I used to come out early when everything's still so quiet and peaceful. I had this idea about seeing the sunrise." He gave a short laugh. "But it was a helluva lot darker out here than I remembered, and when I hit a patch of loose rocks along the trail… Next thing I knew I was rolling down the side of this ravine, and then everything really went dark."

A sheepish expression on his face, he added, "It was stupid, I know, not to have left a note to tell Amy where I was going and… Oh, God. Amy must be thinking the worst."

"She was worried," Zeke confirmed, "but she's going to be so happy that you're safe and sound."

"I really am, you know," the vet said, looking from Zeke to Mollie and back again. "That's why I wanted to come out here at sunrise. Because it feels like I've got this fresh start. A new lease—" he grinned as he looked over at Arti "—or maybe it's a new *leash* on life."

Zeke chuckled at the corny pun. "I'm sure Amy will be thrilled to hear that." Glancing over at Mollie, he said, "Cell service should be better once you're out of the reserve."

"I'll call Amy and call for an ambulance, as well," she said over Bobby's protests that he could make it out on his own.

Pushing to his feet, Zeke handed her another bottle of water. He smiled at her, but she could still see the shadows lingering in his eyes. "Take Arti with you to make sure you can find your way."

Mollie nodded even though she knew her heart would always find its way back to Zeke. But once she told him the truth, she would be the one suffering from the greatest loss. She was going to lose Zeke's friendship. She was going to lose Zeke. She was going to lose…everything.

Twenty minutes later, Zeke followed the emergency responders up the incline. He'd filled them in on Bobby's vitals since he and Mollie had found the other man. The blue-uniformed EMTs were more than capable. They'd stabilized Bobby's left leg in an air cast before transferring him to a stretcher—despite the vet's complaints—and maneuvering their way back up the ravine. Even so, it wasn't easy for Zeke to take a step back. He felt responsible for Bobby.

He felt responsible. Period.

What happened to Patrick was not your fault.

He'd felt certain that once Mollie knew the truth, she would hate him for failing her brother. And yet, what had she done? She'd not only forgiven him, but she'd reassured him that there was nothing to forgive.

Zeke closed his eyes for a moment, picturing the future his friend had been planning. Mollie and Patrick working together, expanding her business, training more dogs like Arti, helping more people like Bobby...

All of it sounded like just the kind of thing Patrick would have lived for.

Was Mollie right? Had only a cruel twist of fate— something beyond Patrick's control, something beyond *Zeke's* control—robbed Patrick of that future?

"Zeke..."

He opened his eyes to find Mollie standing in front of him. She had a smudge of dirt across one cheek and the neckline of her T-shirt was darkened with sweat, and he'd never seen a more beautiful sight. But then he noticed the tears shimmering in her blue-green eyes.

"I'm so sorry," she whispered. "All this time, you've been carrying so much guilt... If I had known—"

"I was afraid to tell you, Mollie. Afraid to admit I'd ignored the warning signs that could have meant saving Patrick's life. That last visit, I was so sure something was wrong..."

Zeke longed to let go of the crushing weight he'd carried for so long, but he couldn't. Not when so many questions still remained. "He wasn't himself, Mollie. If he wasn't suffering from depression, then what was it? He was so distant, so closed off. He was my best friend and—"

"He slept with Lilah!"

Mollie's outburst came out of nowhere. A sudden blast echoing out for miles over the giant oaks and maples, the valleys and streams, to hit the mountains and ricochet back with enough force to send Zeke stumbling back a step.

"He…what?"

She lifted her trembling hands to her mouth as if she could recapture the words, but truth was written in her sorrow-filled gaze. "I'm so sorry, Zeke."

"Patrick…and Lilah? No," Zeke denied, even though he didn't know why he bothered. He knew Mollie wouldn't lie to him. Except…what the hell else could he call the past two years of silence? And why did that betrayal—beyond that of his fiancée, beyond that of his best friend since second grade—cut him to the core?

"It's true, Zeke," Mollie told him, her voice as flat and lifeless as the day she'd shown up at his door and told him Patrick was dead. "It was Patrick's first weekend home. The night of the welcome home party my parents threw for him."

Almost against his will, Zeke flashed back to that night. He'd been excited to see Patrick and Mollie. The three of them had always been so close, but since his engagement a few months before, he'd felt Mollie pulling away. He'd thought Patrick's arrival would be just the thing to bring the three of them together again. But right before the party, he and Lilah had had a fight. Not that that was any surprise. The closer they came to the big day, the bigger their fights had gotten. And he remembered that Lilah hadn't wanted to go to the party.

He'd chalked that argument, like all of the others, up to cold feet.

"If it helps at all," Mollie continued in that same flat voice, "Patrick told me Lilah was the only woman he ever loved. She broke up with him when he went into the army instead of following her to Chapel Hill. He never got over her."

"If it helps?" Zeke echoed. "How the hell could that possibly help?"

He'd been months away from walking down the aisle with a woman who had cheated on him with his best friend. God, what if Lilah *hadn't* broken up with him? Would Mollie have still held her tongue and let him promise to love, honor and cherish a woman who'd betrayed her promise and his trust with Patrick standing by his side as his best man?

He took a stumbling step, nearly tripping as his heel hit a loose rock. Humiliation washed over him like a wave and he had to swallow the sickening bile rising up inside him. To think he'd been such a fool! His best friend had been in love with his fiancée and he'd—he'd missed it entirely. How could he have been so blind?

Mollie flinched. "I'm so sorry, Zeke. Everyone wanted to see Patrick as a hero who'd never do anything wrong, and I—maybe I wanted everyone to see him that way, too. But I'm not perfect. I'm just…me. And if I made a mistake in keeping silent, then it was only because I loved my brother." She wiped at the tears streaking her freckled cheeks. "And because I love you."

Standing in front of Zeke, Mollie felt stripped raw. She had no more secrets to tell, no more shields to hide behind. Her every emotion was exposed to a gaze that she'd never thought could be so cold.

"Zeke, please, try to understand—"

"Oh, I understand. I understand that you've lied to me for the past two years. All that time I spent wondering what I'd done, why Lilah left. All those times you told me I deserved better."

"You did," she whispered.

"I deserved the truth, Mollie! I deserved to hear it from you. But you—"

Mollie was saved from hearing how little Zeke thought of her as the EMTs loaded the stretcher into the back of the ambulance. "I'm riding to the hospital with Bobby," Zeke announced without looking at her. "If you talk to Amy, tell her I'll see her there."

The double doors slammed behind him, cutting Mollie off. Arti let out a low, mournful howl, straining at the end of her leash, and everything inside Mollie ached to give in. To let the dog have her lead and for the two of them to run after the ambulance as the emergency vehicle pulled away. Instead, she held her ground and kept a tight grip on the long nylon tether. "Not this time, girl," she whispered.

There would be no more tagging along. Zeke Harper had left her behind…this time for good.

Chapter Fifteen

"I still can't believe it!" Amanda's eyes were wide as she stared at Mollie over the open pint of double-chocolate-chunk ice cream in her hand. Her gaze shot to Claire, seated on the other side of Mollie's kitchen table. "Lilah and Patrick?"

"That is not the part of the story I need you to focus on right now," Mollie muttered around her own spoonful of cookies and cream.

She hadn't planned to spill her guts over a thousand-calorie serving of ice cream, but Claire had been with Matt when Zeke called to let him know they'd found Bobby. Claire had called Amanda, and the two of them had shown up at Mollie's house, ready to celebrate Mollie's and Arti's roles as heroes.

Mollie could barely swallow the cold and creamy dessert around the lump in her throat.

Some hero.

She wouldn't have bothered opening the door to her friends, but they hadn't stopped knocking and Arti hadn't stopped barking and Mollie...

Mollie wiped her knuckles beneath her eye. She couldn't stop crying.

Her friends had taken one look at her tear-streaked face and immediately rushed inside. Claire had made a pot of tea while Amanda plied her with tissues, an arm around Mollie's shaking shoulders as she poured out the whole, horrible story. She'd managed a few swallows of tea, the warm liquid soothing against her aching throat, before Amanda declared something stronger was needed.

Seated at her kitchen table, the three of them dove into the ice cream Mollie fortunately kept in stock. The cold comfort was all she had to look forward to now that Zeke was gone.

"I know, but—wow!" Amanda slumped back in her chair. "I mean, I knew they hooked up back in high school, but I thought it was just a summer fling."

"Not to Patrick...and I'm guessing not to Lilah." She couldn't help thinking that Lilah hadn't gotten over that long-ago relationship any more than her brother had.

"I still can't believe you kept quiet about this for so long," Claire added.

Even though her friend's voice was free of any accusation, Mollie still flinched. "I *wanted* to tell Zeke at first. I was devastated when they got engaged, so the thought of anything breaking them up was enough to have me doing backflips. And if Lilah had slept with any other guy, I probably would have told Zeke in a heartbeat. But because it was Patrick, I didn't say anything. I was afraid of ruining the friendship the three of us had. Patrick was my closest connection to Zeke, and I couldn't risk losing that. I couldn't risk losing him. So, see?" Mollie pushed the pint of ice cream across the table, unable to stomach another bite. Remembering Zeke's reaction was enough to make her nauseous. "Lilah was right. I was being selfish."

"Okay, first, I can't let the phrase 'Lilah was right' go unchallenged in any situation," Amanda argued. "And besides that, you are the least selfish person I know. Look at all the work you do at the shelter. Look at what you did for Bobby."

Claire nodded. "Matt's told me how much having Charlie around has helped Bobby. He also said that you stopped by Veterans Affairs and offered to help match the other vets with shelter animals. Those are not the actions of a selfish person."

"Claire's right. And second, you had no idea how Zeke was feeling or that he blamed himself. If you'd known how he was suffering and still kept quiet, now *that* would have been selfish."

As much as Mollie wanted to believe her friends, she still couldn't let go of the blame. "I should have told him the truth."

"Okay, so let's play what-if."

"What-if?"

Amanda nodded and scooted her chair closer to the table. "You don't think that what happened on his last trip home—with Lilah, with Zeke—had anything to do with Patrick's death, right?"

"Right. I don't know what he was thinking—or *wasn't* thinking—that led him to sleep with Lilah behind Zeke's back, but he wasn't depressed and he certainly wasn't suicidal." That wasn't her brother. He would have fought to the end, and that likely was exactly what he had done. "He wanted to come back home. He was looking forward to life after the army. We talked about that all the time."

"Okay, so what if you had told Zeke what happened that very night? What if Zeke confronted Patrick and Lilah? What if they had this big, nasty fight where they said all kinds of hateful things in the heat of the moment? And then, what if Patrick left, returned to his unit and went on that same mission? How do you think that would have made Zeke feel if his last moments with his friend were marked by all that hurt and anger and betrayal?"

"I never really thought of it like that." Although wasn't that why she hadn't told Zeke about Patrick and Lilah afterward? Because she hadn't wanted to tarnish Zeke's memories of his friend? "I really was trying to protect him."

"Of course you were." Claire reached across the table to take one of Mollie's hands in hers and Amanda followed suit. "That's what you do when you love someone."

Her words had Mollie's eyes filling with tears once more. "I'm sorry, Amanda. You were so sweet to set me up with Josh, and he really is a great guy."

Her friend smiled. "But he's not Zeke, is he?"

"No," Mollie agreed, her voice little more than a whisper.

If Mollie had ever had any doubt that her feelings for Zeke were real and lasting and not just a girlhood crush, she now had her answer. This was love.

Nothing else could hurt so much.

Seated in a back booth at the Grille, Zeke wanted nothing more than to be left alone. He'd even brought along one of his medical reference books, hoping that keeping his nose buried in the massive hardback would discourage anyone from stopping by his table.

In a town like Spring Forest, he should have known better. "Hey, Zeke, how's it going?" Matt asked as he slid uninvited onto the vinyl bench across from Zeke.

"Busy," he muttered, not lifting his gaze even though the letters in front of him might as well have been ants marching across the page from the way the characters blurred and swarmed. He rubbed at his tired eyes, but the words still didn't make sense.

Nothing made sense anymore.

He wouldn't have bothered going into town to eat, but he hadn't been grocery shopping. And he couldn't bear the thought of stepping into his dining room with all the memories of Mollie lingering there so strongly. Just passing by the doorway, he could still see the bright, colorful mix of decorations, the streamers and balloons drifting in and out of his peripheral vision, and Mollie…

The mix of emotions on her lovely face—the laughter and the tears. The husky tremble in her voice as she whispered his name. The sweet promise in her kiss and the feel of her in his arms…

He couldn't eat in that room. Just like he could no longer sleep in his bed, so he'd been camping out on his living room couch most nights. He'd even crashed at his office the day before.

Ignoring the brusque answer and *keep away* vibes, Matt slapped a hand down on the table. "Man, me, too. The doctor wants Bobby to stay off that sprained ankle for another few days, so I've been putting in extra hours covering for him at the shop. So between work, hanging out with my sister and Ellie and the pups, and with the wedding just over six months away, it's been crazy! But a few months ago, who would have thought, right?"

"Right," Zeke echoed hollowly. He wanted to be happy for his friend, he really did, but at the moment the emotion was beyond him. Buried too deep along with what was left of his heart. "That's great, Matt, but right now I'm—"

"Moping?" his friend suggested.

Zeke's mouth dropped but by the time he'd readied a comeback, Matt was waving over a waitress. "I'll take two double cheeseburgers with the works and a side of chili cheese fries."

He shot a pointed look at Zeke who mumbled, "Not hungry."

Heaving a sigh, Matt told the waitress, "My friend will have the same and we'll take a couple of beers."

Slamming the reference book shut, Zeke leaned across the table. "I am not moping."

Matt leaned back against the burgundy vinyl bench and crossed his arms over his well-worn army T-shirt. "Okay, doc, what would you call it?"

"I'm—" Zeke's words stopped short, cut off by the ragged ache in his throat. For a man trained to dig deep into emotions, he refused to diagnose his own. The wound left by the betrayal and lies Mollie had revealed was too raw. "Not moping," he finally finished after a long moment grappling with all the pain and loss he refused to allow himself to feel.

Matt sighed again, but the waitress's arrival with their beers offered Zeke a temporary reprieve. "You know, Claire and Amanda went to see Mollie the other day."

Zeke's hand clenched around the cold bottle. "So?"

"So…she told them what happened. With Patrick and…everything."

"She told them?" he echoed. Lifting the bottle to his lips, he took a swallow of the beer but the cold brew did little to wash the bitter taste from his mouth. All those years of keeping him in the dark only to turn around and spill those same secrets to her friends.

"Yep." As he eyed him over his own raised bottle, Matt murmured, "How does that make you feel?"

Zeke slammed his beer back down on the table hard enough for a bit of foam to bubble over the top. He shot his friend a death glare at the clichéd use of a psychologist's frequently uttered opener. "Seriously?"

Matt chuckled. "Sorry…couldn't help myself." Sobering quickly, he leaned forward, his large, scarred hands wrapped around the beer. "Look, the way I see it, Mollie kept quiet because she wanted to protect you."

By covering for the fact that his fiancée and his best friend had cheated on him? Zeke didn't feel protected. He felt like the world's biggest fool.

"That couldn't have been easy for her, especially since…" Matt cut himself off to take a large swallow of beer.

"Especially since what?" When the other man hesitated, Zeke ground out, "Not really in the mood to have people keeping things from me right now, Matt."

The former army corporal sighed. "Especially since she's crazy about you."

I love you, Zeke…

His hand tightened around the cold bottle. That was one revelation Zeke wished Mollie had kept to herself. No, that wasn't true. He wished—hell, it didn't matter what he wished. None of it would change the reality of what had happened.

He wasn't about to tell Matt that he and Mollie had made love or that he'd been her first. But maybe that info had been passed along to Claire during Mollie's gabfest, too, and was something else his friend already knew. "Mollie's been through a lot with losing Patrick."

All too often he dealt with patients who'd mistaken a physical relationship for an emotional one. No matter how conflicted his feelings for Mollie were at the moment, he should have done a better job of protecting her. Even if it meant protecting her from himself. "She's vulnerable right now. Loving me probably seemed… safe to her."

Until he'd completely lost his temper—something he rarely did with anyone and never with Mollie. He focused his gaze on the label on the beer bottle rather than meeting his friend's gaze across the table.

Matt snorted. "Yeah, right. Listen, if there's one thing being with Claire has taught me, it's that women are far stronger and far braver than any guy is when it comes to love. Mollie wasn't feeling 'vulnerable.' If anything, she was fed up with waiting around for you to open your eyes to see the amazing woman she'd become and finally found the courage to tell you how she really feels. How she's felt about you for *years*."

"What are you talking about?" Zeke still couldn't wrap his mind around the idea that his best friend was in love with him. To think she'd loved him all along? "No." He shook his head hard enough to dislodge the impossible idea from taking root, unable to believe he'd missed something so huge once again. "No, I would have realized if she…"

"I'm pretty sure Mollie knows her own heart better than you. And news flash, doc. You're not a mind reader. You're human, just like the rest of us. You can't know everything."

Zeke leaned across the table and lowered his voice to a rough whisper. "My fiancée cheated on me with my best friend and my other best friend—" He cut off without saying the words he couldn't bring himself to believe. "Those are two pretty big misses." Practically throwing his shoulders against the back of the padded booth, he demanded, "How could I be so blind?"

"Ah," Matt said wisely, as if the one word explained everything, before he tipped his bottle back.

"Ah?" Zeke echoed. "Is there some big takeaway I'm supposed to glean from that?"

"Only that I get it now. This isn't about a broken heart. It's about a bruised ego."

"That's not true," Zeke argued, even though the words lacked any real conviction. "It's more than that. It's—I trusted Lilah and Patrick." And Mollie. He'd trusted Mollie more than anyone. "If I can be that blind to what's going on right under my nose with the woman I was going to marry and my best friend… who's to say it won't happen again?"

Matt shrugged a broad shoulder. "I'll say."

"And you know this how?" If Zeke wasn't a mind reader, he was pretty sure his friend didn't have a crystal ball.

"Because this time, it's Mollie. The woman you're in love with is your best friend."

Zeke choked on a swallow of beer. "I'm not—I mean, sure, I love Mollie, but I'm not *in* love," he insisted, denying all the signs, even as memories flashed in front of him.

The jealousy that had eaten him alive when Mollie went out with Josh Sylvester. The rush of excitement when Arti successfully found Mollie hiding in the woods. And what about the panic that had sent his adrenaline into overdrive when he thought Mollie had fallen from the ladder?

Not to mention the amazing night they'd spent together.

Zeke swore as the realization hit him, leaving him feeling so weak and boneless he was surprised he didn't slide right out of the booth and fall flat on the floor. He was in love with Mollie McFadden.

"This wasn't supposed to happen," he muttered helplessly.

Matt smirked a little as he clinked his bottle against Zeke's. "You're lucky it did. Mollie's an amazing woman. One who would do anything to protect you... including bear the burden of a secret that was never hers to keep."

This time, it's Mollie.

The words echoed through Zeke's thoughts after he'd said goodbye to Matt and left the Grille. Circling around in his mind long enough for him to finally recognize they weren't quite right.

It had *always* been Mollie.

Other women had come and gone from his life, leaving no lasting marks on the terrain of his heart. Somehow, without his realizing, Mollie had already etched a permanent place there, and nothing and no one was going to smooth over the deep grooves.

All of which made the secret she'd kept from him so much harder to bear.

He'd planned to go back home but soon found himself heading out of town, not stopping until he'd reached the wrought-iron gates of Spring Forest's cemetery. He'd been to visit Patrick's grave several times during the past two years but always with Mollie.

As he parked the car and made his way across the lush lawn to the familiar plot without her by his side, he expected to feel alone. He didn't. Instead, for the first time in a long time, he felt Patrick's presence beside him.

He gazed at the name and dates etched into the white marble. *Beloved son, brother and friend who gave his life in defense of his country.*

His grave, along with many in the surrounding verdant hills, was marked with a small flag in honor of the upcoming day of remembrance. The red, white and blue waved in the late afternoon breeze, testament to all those who had served.

Everyone wanted to see Patrick as a hero.

"You could be a real SOB sometimes, you know that?"

His mother had raised him to think first, to keep his mouth shut if he didn't have something nice to say, and to never, ever speak ill of the dead. If she'd been standing by his side, she would have told him off. But the sound he heard in the wind whispering through the stately oaks lining the cemetery was not his mother's scolding.

It was Patrick's laughter.

"You cheated at cards." His voice gained strength as he went on. "You were the dirtiest basketball player on the court. You were a *lousy* drunk, and I swear to God, you still owe me that fifty bucks you borrowed when we went down to that music fest in Charleston."

After the words rushed out, Zeke sucked in the first deep breath he'd taken in months, it seemed. Maybe years. The raw honesty left him aching, even though the statements were completely true and nothing he hadn't said right to his friend's face before.

But the ache inside wasn't from what he'd said. Instead it was from what he'd left unsaid. Sucking in another deep breath, he exhaled and let go of the burden he had carried since the day his friend died. "Not a day goes by that I don't miss you…" Buoyed on the same breeze that rippled over the tiny flags, his words drifted across the silent cemetery. "And I forgive you."

Mollie squinted as she gazed out across the dog park. Even hiding behind a pair of large-framed sunglasses, her eyes felt overly sensitive and too exposed to the bright summer day. Of course, that probably had more to do with the buckets of tears she'd cried the past several days than the midmorning sun.

She would have liked nothing more than to stay in bed with the covers pulled over her head, shutting out the rest of the world for, well, the rest of her life. But, unfortunately for her, her dogs didn't give her that luxury. They still needed to be fed and groomed and walked, which meant Mollie also managed to feed and groom and walk herself, even if none of those efforts met with one hundred percent success.

She was officially out of ice cream, dressed in some of her oldest clothes, and she'd agreed to meet a new client only because the Whitaker sisters had begged her to.

"We've just had a nice young man adopt a dog from us this morning," Birdie had explained.

And Bunny had added, "The woman he's in love with is a dog lover and…well, he's in somewhat over his head. He could use your help."

Mollie wanted to say no. A head over heels in love client? Not exactly someone she wanted to take on, but her dedication to Furever Paws and the shelter pups surpassed her own heartbreak. She could return to wallowing after giving this new pet owner a remedial training session.

Zeke hadn't called or texted her since riding off with Bobby in the ambulance, and she was starting to wonder if he ever would. Spring Forest was a small town and they knew all the same people, so they were bound to run into each other eventually.

Bad enough she couldn't go anywhere without some memory of Zeke pouring salt on the open wound of her heart. The thought of seeing him again, of seeing the hurt and anger and betrayal reflected in his hazel eyes again, was enough to make Mollie want to pull her own disappearing act. But running off to Europe wasn't exactly feasible when her dogs, her business, her friends and even her parents were all in Spring Forest.

She would have to find a way to move forward on her own. Without Patrick. Without Zeke.

As she watched the dogs romping in the yard, a small tan pup broke away from the pack and raced toward her. As the dog drew near, she recognized the short-legged chiweenie. Despite the tears blurring her vision, she managed a smile as she knelt down to greet a familiar friend.

"Hey, Tucker." She laughed a little as the dog jumped up to give her a quick lick on the chin. Tucker had been a long-time Furever Paws resident until he'd been adopted by Ryan Carter for his son, Dillon.

"Honestly, Tucker," Ryan said as he walked across the grassy park toward Mollie, "is that any way to greet a lady?"

"He's just saying hi to an old friend," she said as she gave the small dog a quick scratch on his back, setting his slender tail off and wagging. Pushing to her feet, she greeted Amanda's fiancé. "Are Amanda and Dillon here with you?"

"No, Dillon's spending the weekend with my former in-laws and Amanda's checking out the fresh fruits and vegetables at The Granary, so this guy and I are on our own this morning."

"Well, it's a great day for hanging out at the park together."

"It is, and I'm glad to run into you. I was planning to give you a call later today."

"Oh?" Glancing down at Tucker, who was sitting like a perfect gentleman and seemed to be smiling so innocently up at her, she asked, "Are you needing some help with this guy?" At one time, Tucker had been a little on the standoffish side and rather particular about his humans, which had led to his return to the shelter after failing to connect with his adoptive families. But Dillon and the small dog had bonded from the start.

"No, not at all. Tucker's been great for Dillon. It's actually Arti I want to talk to you about. I'd like to do a story on the two of you."

"You want to interview me?"

Ryan smiled. "Well, as much as I'd like to interview Arti, I think the readers would get more out of one with you." Turning serious, he said, "Amanda filled me in on how the two of you found Bobby Doyle. It would make a great feature for the *Chronicle*."

"Really?"

"Our readership took a real interest in the stories we've done covering the shelter, how it was damaged by the storm and how the community came together to donate money at last month's fund-raiser. I think they'd really be interested in learning how you took a shelter dog and turned her into, well, a super dog." Ryan gave her a kind smile, as if recognizing how uncomfortable she was with the thought of being in the spotlight. "You helped saved the day, Mollie."

Mollie opened her mouth, ready with a quick denial. After all, her brother was the hero in the family, while she'd been nothing more than little Mollie McFadden, Patrick's tagalong sister.

Almost as if reading her mind, Tucker gave a sudden bark. Mollie looked down at the small dog sitting so patiently at her feet and thought of how much he'd helped Dillon. She thought of Arti, and Charlie and three-legged Hank. All dogs who had been abandoned or rejected or ignored and yet had gone on to make huge differences in the lives of the humans around them.

There were all kinds of heroes, and maybe, just maybe, she needed to start believing that little Mollie McFadden could be one of them.

Meeting Ryan's gaze, she said, "I'll do the interview. I'd also like to let people know about a joint venture between the shelter and the veterans' support group. We're calling it Pets for Vets, matching veterans with homeless animals—either as fosters or potential adopters."

Mollie had run the idea by the Whitaker sisters and both women were fully on board. In some cases, Mollie would work with the vets to train the dogs for service. In other cases, the dogs would simply offer the companionship of a loving, loyal, four-legged friend.

Ryan's eyes lit as she discussed the new program. "That sounds like a great idea, and one that certainly deserves media attention."

After setting up a time for the interview, Ryan and Tucker went on their way.

Mollie wished they had stayed longer. It was easier to ignore the pain inside her when someone else was around. Maybe she'd look into fostering another dog soon. She'd already called the Whitaker sisters to tell them she was a foster failure when it came to Chief. The once-shy shepherd, who'd taken to cuddling up with her at night, was more than ready for adoption, but Mollie wasn't anywhere close to letting him go.

A high-pitched bark distracted her from her thoughts. Spotting a black Lab puppy running her way, tongue and tail flying, feet way too big for its tiny body, she managed her first real smile since Zeke had surprised her with his holiday mash-up at his house. The pup skidded to a stop inches from her legs only to instantly pounce on her shoelaces.

Chuckling a bit, Mollie bent down to rub a hand over the silky head. "Hey, sweetie, what's your name?"

"Her name's Midnight."

Mollie froze at the familiar voice, her fingers sinking into the dog's soft fur. She pushed to her feet slowly, keeping her gaze focused on the destroyer of shoelaces. She swallowed hard. She'd known she would run into Zeke sometime, but she didn't imagine that the first words out of her mouth would be, "You adopted a puppy?"

"Yeah," he said, his voice slightly gruff, "I did."

"That's a big responsibility."

"That's what I thought, too, but I've recently figured out I was wrong. It's not about responsibility. It's about love."

At that, Mollie couldn't stop herself from looking up at him. He was more gorgeous than ever to her starved senses. Her heart ached a little to see one of her royal blue Best Friends T-shirts hugging his wide shoulders in a way she could only dream of doing. The midmorning breeze ruffled his chestnut hair, and her hands clenched into fists of longing at her sides.

"You said I needed a new best friend," he reminded her. "Although those are some really big shoes for such a tiny puppy to fill."

Grateful for the shades hiding her eyes, Mollie blinked back tears. "Patrick was—"

"My friend," Zeke filled in as he stepped close enough for her to breathe in the familiar scent of his aftershave. "But I wasn't talking about Patrick. You, Mollie. You're my best friend. You have been for years. I was just too blind to see it."

Though Mollie was grateful that Zeke seemed to have forgiven her for the secret she'd kept, friendship was no longer enough for her. Not after finally admitting she was in love with him. Not after finally making love with him.

Staring out across the dog park, Mollie locked in on a small family. A dark-haired man was laughing as a little boy chased a Jack Russell puppy—or maybe it was the other way around as the two of them ran in circles. A blonde woman, standing in the shade of one of the leafy oaks lining the park, called out encouragement as the boy and his dog stumbled over their own feet and each other before the little guy finally plopped down on his backside. The childish giggles and high-pitched barks drifting on the summer breeze went straight to the ache in her chest.

"I can't—I can't do this, Zeke." She'd told him that nothing would change their friendship, but she'd lied about that, too. She couldn't go back to the way things had been. Not just because their relationship had changed, but because *she'd* changed.

No more tagging along.

She would choose her own path and had already taken steps in the right direction with her idea for Pets for Vets as well as reaching out to local law enforcement to talk with them about training more dogs for search and rescue work. This time, she was moving on.

"Please, Mollie," Zeke asked, his voice ragged with emotion. "Give me another chance."

As if sensing his distress, the puppy whimpered and jumped up against his jean-clad legs. Bending down, he scooped the dog into his arms where she panted happily against his chest, her pink tongue hanging out to one side. "You said you loved me."

Oh, God. Mollie's eyes burned. Was he going to use that against her, too? As if the sight of him cradling the adorable puppy wasn't enough to tear her to pieces. "Zeke—"

"I love you."

The ragged edges of her heart ripped open wider. He loved her. Of course he did. As the little sister he never wanted. As his best friend. "I can't…"

"I love you, Mollie," he insisted. "I love every stubborn, hardheaded, frustrating part of you. I love how you put your dogs in front of everything. I love how hard you fought to protect Patrick's memory, and I love how you protected me. But mostly I love the idea of spending the rest of my life with my best friend."

She was dreaming. She had to be dreaming. After so many years of imagining Zeke declaring his love for her—and where better than at a dog park?—she couldn't believe that dream was coming true. But if she was still alone in bed with only Chief snuggled up beside her, well, then she didn't ever want to wake up.

"You're wrong," she said finally and watched his

face fall, but only for a second before she stepped close enough to wrap her arms around his waist with the puppy cradled between them. "My dogs don't come first. It's, well, it's more like a tie."

"I'll take that," Zeke vowed with a rough laugh as he bent his head toward her. "Patrick said you always had the biggest heart. As long as there's room for me, I don't mind sharing that space with a couple of dogs."

Thinking of her decision to adopt Chief, Mollie asked, "What do you think about three?"

"I think three sounds perfect." His hazel eyes filled with emotion, he murmured, "I'm sorry, Mollie. Sorry I didn't see what was right in front of me this whole time. It was you. I should have known it was you."

"It doesn't matter what happened before. We're here now. Right where we're supposed to be. And I love you."

"I should probably wait until I have a ring, but I feel like I've wasted so much time already." Taking a deep breath as he brushed the hair back from her face, he asked, "Mollie McFadden, will you and Arti and Chief marry me and Midnight?"

"Oh, Zeke!" Laughter and tears bubbled up inside her at the perfect proposal. As she threw her arms around his neck, the puppy squirmed between them with an excited yelp. "You brought me a dog! Who needs a diamond?"

"So, is that a yes?"

"Yes! Of course, it's yes!"

Standing in his arms with a dozen or so dogs barking and racing around them on the lush green grass, Zeke lowered his head to kiss her. A kiss that took them beyond best friends toward a future filled with love and laughter...and dogs.

Epilogue

Memorial Day dawned beautiful and bright. The sun shone in the blue skies overhead. Wisps of fluffy clouds offered a bit of shade and a warm breeze drifted through the flags waved by the crowds on either side of Main Street. From what Mollie could see, most of Spring Forest had turned out for the parade.

Families lined the sidewalks in front of the brick buildings that made up the heart of downtown. The high school band marched by, playing a medley of patriotic songs. The volunteer fire department rode by on engine number 49 followed by a few police officers on horseback. But the highlight of the event was the march of the veterans, resplendent in their full uniforms, gold buttons, medals and ribbons gleaming in the sun. Younger soldiers from recent conflicts marched side by side with aging veterans from previous wars, including a few who'd served all the way back in World War II.

Standing on the corner in front of Whole Bean, Mollie sang and cheered and cried, especially when she saw Matt with his dog Hank and Bobby walking with Charlie at his heel. She didn't have to say a word for Zeke, standing close behind her, to wrap his arms around her and draw her tight to his chest. Even her parents appeared both moved and pleased by the tribute.

"That was a lovely parade," Georgia McFadden said, surreptitiously wiping a tear from the corner of her eye. "Patrick would have been proud."

"Yes," Zeke agreed, "and you should be very proud of him."

No lingering guilt, bitterness or anger colored his words. Standing next to him on that May morning, the red, white and blue flags flying all around them, Mollie loved Zeke even more than she'd thought possible. And just when the day couldn't get any better, her mother turned to her with a slight smile.

"We're proud of both of our children," she said before she and Mollie's father excused themselves.

"Wow," Mollie said as she blinked back even more tears. Turning to Zeke, looking so handsome in a button-down blue checked shirt and dark denim jeans, she cupped a hand at the back of his neck and urged his head down for a tender kiss. "Thank you," she told her soon-to-be husband.

She knew no one would ever take Patrick's place, not in her life and not in her parents', but knowing that their son's best friend would soon be their son-in-law had started to heal something inside them. And while Zeke insisted his recent conversations with the McFaddens had been nothing more than a way of getting to know his future in-laws, Mollie knew he was helping them move past their grief and anger as only he could.

"Me?" His expression filled with enough love to take her breath away, he brushed the lingering tears from her eyes. "No way, Mollie, that was all you. The article Ryan wrote about you in the *Chronicle* really opened your parents' eyes."

The pleasure and pride in his smile heated Mollie's cheeks. She was still somewhat embarrassed by her sudden fame. The feature, which had spotlighted the veterans and the foster dogs, also focused on Mollie and the work she'd done with Arti. She was glad the publicity had drawn attention to the shelter as well as her own business, but wasn't quite comfortable being in the limelight herself.

Still, Zeke was right. The article, along with her engagement, had broken down some of the barriers to the point where her parents had hosted an engagement party for them. A party that had included Arti, Chief and Midnight.

Mollie was glad her parents had started to accept both her career and her pets. The dogs had played such big roles in her romance with Zeke, neither of them could imagine life without them. But she was going to wait a little longer before telling her mother that they planned to have Arti and Midnight as flower girls and Chief for their ring bearer at the wedding.

As much as she was looking forward to the ceremony, her heart still ached for the big brother who wouldn't be there to see her marry his best friend. But Patrick would have wanted her to be happy each and every day, and especially on her wedding day. And even though he might not be there in body, he was always with her in spirit. Always looking out for her...

"Did you know my brother warned all the guys in

Spring Forest to stay away from me before he left for boot camp?"

Zeke chuckled at that. "Feeling like you missed out?"

"No!" Slapping at his shoulder, she said, "You were the only guy I ever wanted. I was just wondering if you knew."

"Yeah, Patrick made it pretty clear you were hands-off."

"So he scared you off, too?" she challenged with a lift to her eyebrow.

"No." Zeke laughed again before turning serious. Taking her hand in his, he ran his thumb over her knuckles, stopping at the diamond engagement ring. "Actually, he never told me to stay away. He asked me to look out for you. He said you had the biggest heart of anyone he knew."

"He asked you to protect it," she whispered.

"And I promise to spend the rest of my life doing just that," he vowed as he lifted her hand to press a kiss to the center of her palm. "Although I don't know if our getting married is quite what he had in mind."

"Don't be so sure," she told him as she caressed his cheek with her fingertips.

After all, her brother had known the two of them better than anyone.

As a confetti popper launched a flurry of red, white and blue streamers all around, and as Zeke kissed her beneath the bright blue skies, Mollie couldn't help thinking Sergeant First Class Patrick McFadden had completed his final mission.

* * * * *

*Look for the next book in Furever Yours
the new Special Edition continuity,*

The Nanny Clause

By USA TODAY *bestselling author
Karen Rose Smith
On sale April 2019, wherever Harlequin books
and ebooks are sold.*

And fetch the previous Furever Yours tales!

A New Leash on Love
by Melissa Senate

How to Rescue a Family
by Teri Wilson

Available now!

Shania flushed as she raised her eyes toward Daniel. "I don't usually babble like this."

Daniel found the pink hue that had suddenly risen to her cheeks rather sweet. The next second, he realized that he was staring. Daniel forced himself to look away. "I hadn't noticed."

"Yes, you had," Shania contradicted. "But I think that it's very nice of you to pretend that you hadn't." When she heard Daniel laugh softly to himself, she asked him, "What's so funny?" before she could think to stop herself.

"I'm not accustomed to hearing the word *nice* used to describe me," he admitted.

Didn't the man have any close friends? Someone to bolster him up when he was down on himself? "You're kidding."

The lopsided smile answered her before he did. "Something else I'm not known for."

She pretended that he was a student and she did a quick assessment of the man before her. "You know you're being very hard on yourself."

"Not hard," he contradicted. "Just honest."

She had no intention of letting this slide. If he had been one of her students, she would have done what she could to raise his spirits—or maybe it was his self-esteem that needed help.

"Well, I think you're nice—and you do have a sense of humor."

"If you say so," Daniel replied, not about to dispute the matter. He had a feeling that arguing with Shania would be pointless. "But just so you know, I'm not about to chuck my career and become a stand-up comedian."

She grinned at his words. "See, I told you that you had a sense of humor," she declared happily.

Don't miss
The Lawman's Romance Lesson *by Marie Ferrarella,*
available April 2019 wherever
Harlequin® *Special Edition books and ebooks are sold.*

www.Harlequin.com

They'd both just turned back to their work when a familiar loud, croaking sound cut the silence.

The twins shrieked and ran from where they'd been playing into the little cabin's yard and slammed into Anna, their faces frightened.

"What was that?" Anna sounded alarmed, too, kneeling to hold and comfort both girls.

"Nothing to be afraid of," Sean said, trying to hold back laughter. "It's just egrets. Type of water bird." He located the source of the sound, then went over to the trio, knelt beside them, and pointed through the trees and growth.

When the girls saw the stately white birds, they gasped.

"They're so pretty!" Anna said.

"Pretty?" Sean chuckled. "Nobody from around here would get excited about an egret, nor think it's especially pretty." But as he watched another one land beside the first, white wings spread wide as it skidded into the shallow water, he realized that there was beauty there. He just hadn't noticed it before.

That was what kids did for you: made you see the world through their fresh, innocent eyes. A fist of longing clutched inside his chest.

The twins were tugging at Anna's shirt now, trying to get her to take them over toward the birds. "You may go look as long as you can see me," she said, "but take careful steps by the water." She took the bolder twin's face in her hands. "The water's not deep, but I still don't want you to wade in. Do you understand?"

Both little girls nodded vigorously.

They ran off and she watched for a few seconds, then turned back to her work with a barely audible sigh.

"Go take a look with them," he urged her. "It's not every day kids see an egret for the first time."

"You're sure?"

"Go on." He watched her run like a kid over to her girls. And then he couldn't resist walking a few steps closer and watching them, shielded by the trees and brush.

The twins were so excited that they weren't remembering to be quiet. "It caught a *fish*!" the one was crowing, pointing at the bird, which, indeed, held a squirming fish in its mouth.

"That one's neck is like an S!" The quieter twin squatted down, rapt.

Anna eased down onto the sandy beach, obviously unworried about her or the girls getting wet or dirty, laughing and talking to them and sharing their excitement.

The sight of it gave him a melancholy twinge. His own mom had been a nature lover. She'd taken him and his brothers fishing, visited a nature reserve a few times, back in Alabama where they'd lived before coming here.

Oh, if things were different, he'd run with this, see where it led…

Don't miss
Lee Tobin McClain's Low Country Hero, *available March 2019 from HQN Books!*

www.Harlequin.com

Copyright © 2019 by Lee Tobin McClain